'So, are you gonna go out with him?'

'Exhilarating sequel to *the crew* . . . unflinching and authentic'
Publishing News

www.kidsatrandomhouse.co.uk

Also available by Bali Rai:

(un)arranged marriage

the crew

Rani and Sukh

The Whisper

www.balirai.com

THE LAST TABOO

BALI RAI

CORGI BOOKS

R 12412
(f)

THE LAST TABOO
A CORGI BOOK 978 0 552 55301 8

Published in Great Britain by Corgi Books,
an imprint of Random House Children's Books

This edition published 2006

5 7 9 10 8 6 4

Corgi Books are published by Random House Children's Books,
61–63 Uxbridge Road, London W5 5SA,
a division of The Random House Group Ltd

Addresses for companies within The Random House Group Limited
can be found at: www.randomhouse.co.uk/offices.htm

The Random House Group Limited supports The Forest Stewardship
Council (FSC), the leading international forest certification organisation.
All our titles that are printed on Greenpeace approved FSC certified paper
carry the FSC logo. Our paper procurement policy can be found at:
www.rbooks.co.uk/environment.

Set in 12/14.5pt Bembo Schoolbook

THE RANDOM HOUSE GROUP Limited Reg. No. 954009

www.kidsatrandomhouse.co.uk

A CIP catalogue record for this book is available from the British Library.

Printed and bound in Great Britain by
Cox & Wyman Ltd, Reading, Berkshire

I'd like to thank the following people for their hard work and support: Penny Luithlen; Lucy Walker, Annie Eaton and the rest of the RHCB crew; John and Vivian at the Newham Bookshop; Browsers Bookshop in Leicester and everyone else who's helped along the way.

And to all the schools, librarians, pupils and teachers who I've met in the last five years – thank you.

SIMRAN

The first time I noticed Tyrone he was trying to get out of a fight with some lads who went to my school. Tyrone's school was about half a mile from ours, and the lads from the two schools were *always* fighting, just like the immature little shits they were. Tyrone was waving his hands in the air, explaining something to a gang of Asian lads who called themselves the Desi Posse. The idiot who thought he ran the gang, Rajinder Mann, was arguing back.

As I stood watching with my best friend Lisa, I was sure Tyrone would get beaten up. But in the end it all seemed to fade away, all the macho bullshit and the peacock-like posturing. Just like a sudden shower disappears as sunshine breaks through the clouds. The lads were little boys playing at being men, as Lisa described it. All the pushing and name-calling, the anger – all of it seemed fake, like they were just butting heads – or at least that's what I thought. In the end I watched as Tyrone walked off with a slight swagger, and wondered why I'd never noticed him before. He was gorgeous.

'They're all freaks,' Lisa said as we walked back to school.

'Not all of them,' I replied.

Lisa shook her head and stood firm in her argument. '*All* of them,' she repeated.

'But that lad they were arguing with – he doesn't go to our school, so how do you *know* he's a freak?' I asked.

'Because he has a penis,' Lisa said, like it was the gospel truth.

'You sound like a nutter yourself,' I told her.

She shrugged and told me that she'd rather be a nutter than a stupid macho boy with sexual orientation issues.

'They all want to shag each other,' she told me. 'The fighting, that's all foreplay – they just don't know it yet.'

I gave her a funny look but ignored what she said. 'Wonder what his name was,' I said.

'Whose name?'

'That lad – the black lad the Desi Posse were pickin' on . . .' I said.

'Tyrone,' Lisa told me, as she avoided a Year Seven lad who had run into her path. 'Little shit!'

'How'd you know that?' I asked, watching her clout the poor kid round the back of the head. He looked at her, swore and ran off.

'Just seen him from around – that's all,' she replied, ignoring what had just happened.

'Oh,' I said, before changing the subject slightly. 'What do you think they were arguing about?'

'Who cares?' Lisa said, flatly. 'With that gang it's usually something stupid.'

'Yeah – I guess you're right,' I said.

I honestly didn't give Tyrone any more thought after that. At least not for a few weeks. There were two other schools within a mile radius of ours, which meant that every few weeks there was some kind of fight or run-in. It was a strange thing to do – to put so many teenagers together in such a small area – but thanks to that lack of town planning I didn't have to wait long for my next glimpse of Tyrone. Although it was in the worst of circumstances . . .

It was a Wednesday afternoon and school had just finished. As I made my way out of the grounds with Lisa I noticed that there seemed to be a lot of people just hanging about on the street. And I mean a *lot* of people. Some of the residents were standing outside their houses too, as though they were expecting trouble. They must have had access to a crystal ball because suddenly a scream went up and then two gangs of lads crashed into each other, like angry waves across a concrete and tarmac sea.

Lisa pulled me to one side as some of the Desi Posse barged past, one lad pulling out a thick wooden stick and holding it above his head. They waded in and began to throw wild punches and kicks. And in the midst of all the fighting I saw Tyrone, ducking and weaving and throwing punches of his own. I watched him until he disappeared into the mass of bodies.

'Let's get out of here!' shouted Lisa, as the other kids began to scatter.

I stood where I was, frozen to the spot, watching the

fighting. It was the biggest fight I had ever seen, with about forty lads from each school going at it. There was something strange about it too, apart from the fact that they were just charging at each other like bulls; something else that I couldn't quite work out. I turned to Lisa, who looked angry rather than scared.

'We're gonna get battered for this,' she said.

I shrugged. 'We aren't doing anything.'

'It doesn't matter,' Lisa told me. 'When the shit hits the fan it's going to affect us all . . .'

'They're all mad,' I said, watching as a lad from the Desi smashed a bottle into another boy's head. I flinched and looked away, feeling sick.

'We can't just stand here,' said Lisa.

I told her to wait. 'We're surrounded by them,' I pointed out.

At first I hadn't noticed but when I looked round I saw that the fight was spilling over towards us really fast. I flinched as Lisa ducked and a chair leg went flying past her head.

'*Shit!*' she shouted, getting angry.

Then I saw a couple of teachers run out of the main building towards the fight. One of the teachers, Mr Brown, grabbed a couple of boys, scuffling with them, but they were trying to get away, throwing punches and swear words at him in equal measure. His face turned lobster red and he fell to the ground, clutching at his chest. A girl, the nearest one to Mr Brown, screamed and began to sob as the flashing lights and wailing sirens of police cars came nearer, making my head throb. Pupils started to run everywhere as the police officers tried to round them up.

Lisa gave me a tug. 'Come on!' she shouted, pulling me back into the school grounds.

'Let's take the back exit by the car park,' I said.

We ran past more teachers coming the other way and then down into the staff and visitors' car park. The gate was open and we made our way out into the side street, only to be called back by Mrs Clarke, a maths teacher.

'*Girls!*'

We turned to see her standing with a policewoman, her face red.

'Please make your way back into school,' she insisted.

'But we were goin' home,' said Lisa.

'We didn't *see* anything,' I lied.

'It doesn't matter,' the policewoman said. 'You still have to come back.'

Lisa swore before we trudged slowly back into school, the aftermath of the fight all around us. And even then I couldn't stop thinking about Tyrone, hoping that he was OK – which is a pretty strange thing to do, given the circumstances.

In the end we didn't get home until well after seven. Everyone who had seen the fight had to give statements, as rumours flew round about Mr Brown and two or three pupils being killed. They were all wrong, though not by much. It turned out that Mr Brown had been stabbed and was seriously injured. Two lads from our school also had stab wounds, and six from the other school, City, had serious injuries too. And one of the residents, who had tried to stop the fighting, had collapsed from a heart attack.

My dad, who'd picked me and Lisa up from school, shook his head on the way home.

'This is bad,' he told us – it was kind of stating the obvious.

'We know,' I replied. 'We *did* see it all.'

'If anyone dies because of the—' he began, but I cut him off.

'Was David involved?' I asked.

My dad shook his head. 'I rang his mobile,' he told me. 'He was bunking off with Dean.'

I felt relieved. My brother David and his best mate, Dean, weren't exactly good at staying out of trouble.

'You OK, Lisa?' my dad asked.

'Yes, Mr Gill – I'm fine,' she replied.

'And your mum . . . ?' he asked.

'She's OK.'

'Well, give her my regards.'

'I will,' replied Lisa, as my dad pulled up outside her house.

'See you later,' I told her.

'OK, babes – call me,' she replied, smiling weakly at me.

SIMRAN

The school stayed closed for nearly a week as the media swooped and reports of a race riot began to appear in the national newspapers. I wondered what they meant about race until I realized that they were right. That was the strange thing that I couldn't work out when the fighting was going on. All the lads from our school had been Asian; the others had been white or black.

'That's just stupid media hype,' Lisa said on the other end of the phone when I read her one of the newspaper stories.

'But it's true,' I pointed out. 'The gang from our school *was* all Asian . . .'

'That's because our school is *seventy per cent* Asian,' Lisa told me. 'I'm in a minority here. And it *was* the Desi Posse fightin' – you *have* to be Asian to be in it.'

'But that makes it racial,' I said.

Lisa sighed. 'Sim, the only way it would be a race riot

7

is if the gangs hated each other over skin colour. They just hate each other period – it's that macho, school rivalry thing . . .'

'I'm not so sure . . .'

'Well, let's wait and see,' said Lisa. 'If there's more to it, it'll soon come out.'

You know when people say things and then you forget about them? And then, months or years later, what they said comes into your mind? That was what would eventually happen with Lisa's comment.

'So what we gonna do while school is closed?' I asked her.

'Dunno. We could go into town tomorrow . . .'

'There's a film on that I wanna watch,' I said.

'OK,' said Lisa. 'And before that you can help me choose some make-up.'

'Sounds great,' I replied, smiling.

It was while I was waiting for Lisa outside a shoe shop that I first spoke to Tyrone. I saw him walking over with a friend. I looked up, hoping he'd notice me, and he did. He smiled and asked if I was the same girl he'd seen on the way to school a few times. I shrugged, secretly relieved that he hadn't been hurt in the fight I'd witnessed.

'Could be,' I said, smiling back.

'You go to Hills – down the road from mine . . .' he said.

I nodded, feeling my hand reach up to my left cheek of its own accord and touch the place where I'd had a spot only a few days earlier.

'So, you got a name, sister?' he asked.

'Simran,' I told him, dropping my hand and hoping I hadn't drawn attention to it.

'I'm Tyrone,' he said, before looking at his friend, 'and this here is I'm Going.'

He grinned at me. His friend nodded and said that he was going to check out some new trainers at JD Sports.

'See? I told you he was going . . .' he said.

'But why did he leave?' I asked.

'So that I could chat to you on my own – maybe take you for a coffee,' he told me.

'I can't – I'm waiting for a friend . . .'

'Male or female?' he asked, raising an eyebrow.

'Female – not that it's any of your business,' I replied.

'You got a man?'

I smiled. 'That's very forward,' I said, teasing him.

'I *am* very forward, sister,' he told me. 'So, you gonna answer or not?'

'Er . . . put it this way: I'm not looking for a boyfriend.'

Tyrone smiled at me, his face lighting up. 'Just one date, sister. That's all I'm askin' . . .'

I shook my head, trying not to stare at him. He was gorgeous, with his beautiful smile and his deep chocolate-brown skin. But I didn't want to go out with him.

'Sorry, I'm not looking for a boyfriend,' I said again.

'Yeah, but—'

'Sorry,' I repeated.

'You're harsh, man. Buff, but harsh,' he told me with another grin, his eyes sparkling like diamonds.

'I've gotta go,' I said, as I spotted Lisa walking towards me.

'OK, but I'll see you around . . .' he replied, like it was bound to happen.

I turned and walked towards Lisa, trying not to look back but failing miserably, sad cow that I am. I just had to turn round. And when I did, he was still standing in the same place, grinning at me. Stupid boy.

'Who's that?' asked Lisa.

'I thought you knew who he was,' I replied.

Lisa squinted at him. 'Oh, him,' she said. 'Tyrone . . . I haven't got my lenses in today – sorry.'

'Blind girl.'

Lisa smiled. 'So what did he want?' she asked me.

'Not a lot. Just chatting me up . . .' I told her.

'He was at that fight, wasn't he?' she said.

'Yeah – I told you I saw him, but only very briefly,' I replied, trying to make it sound like nothing. He was so fit – I didn't want Lisa to not like him.

'He was still *there*,' she said. 'Although he's kinda cute, isn't he?'

'Yeah,' I said.

'Simmy's got a boyfriend!' teased Lisa, chanting childishly.

'No I haven't!' I protested.

She laughed. 'Not yet.'

'I'm serious,' I told her. 'I'm not sure I can go out with him.'

'Why not?' she asked me.

I didn't know what to say to her. The reason was that Tyrone was black and I wasn't sure how my family would react. But I didn't want her to think that I was some kind of racist so I changed the subject – not that Lisa even cared.

'I saw some amazing shoes in that shop back there,' I said.

Both of Lisa's eyebrows rose up her forehead. 'Pray *where* exactly?' she said in a stupid voice. 'And don't *dare* hide them from me – shoes, shoes, shoes . . .'

I grinned and turned to see if Tyrone was still standing in the same spot, but he'd gone. I thought how gorgeous he was, smiled at what he'd said to me, and then followed Lisa.

After spending hours walking round the same shops over and over again, we finally caught the bus home. Lisa lived five doors away from me, in a house very similar to my parents', only ours had four bedrooms, not three, thanks to a box-like extension on the side. It wasn't posh where we lived but it wasn't poor either. It was just nice, in that kind of nondescript way that doesn't actually mean very much at all.

'You coming in?' I asked Lisa as we got to my house.

'Not today, Simmy. I've got a load of stuff to do at home. I'll see you tomorrow, babes.'

'Bye.'

I watched her go, wondering how she'd ended up with a figure that was so much better than mine, the lucky cow, before I headed up my drive, searching my bag for keys.

Jay, my little brother, was watching telly when I went into the living room. 'Hi, sis,' he said, not looking up from his programme.

'Hi . . . where's Mum?'

He shrugged. He was wearing blue shorts and a football

shirt that was too big for him. 'Shops, I think. There ain't no food in.'

'Oh, right. What about David?'

'He's upstairs with Dean – they're on the PlayStation.'

'Typical,' I said to myself.

'They won't let me play either – and they took my football game,' moaned Jay.

'Tell Mum when she gets back,' I told him.

'But . . .'

'*But, but, but . . .*' I mimicked.

'Shit-breath!'

'*Jay!* Who taught you to say that?'

Jay looked at me and grinned. 'No one – I heard Dad say it.'

'Well, don't be using it again.'

'Or what, Sim-card?' he asked, using the stupid nickname he'd made up for me.

'Or I'll show your mates the photos of you from India – the ones where you're taking a bath in the river with your little tickle-tackle out.'

Jay shook his head and went back to watching the telly.

I went up to my room and unpacked my school bag, wondering what time my dad would get in. I looked at a picture of him with my mum, which I had on my desk. It had been taken when they were both eighteen and going out with each other. They both had stupid haircuts and lame clothes but they were smiling like nutters, standing outside a club called Subway. They'd caused a scandal with their 'love marriage', as my extended family called it. My mum was supposed to marry someone else – someone her family had chosen for her. And my dad had actually been engaged to some girl from India. But they were secretly seeing each other. And in the end they ran off together and got married in a registry office.

My dad had been disowned for a few years, until my grandad, who wasn't the one who disowned him, returned from India and talked him back into the family. It still took a while for us all to be accepted by my dad's brothers, but in the end they relented, even if they still slag us off now and then.

I've got two uncles on my dad's side. My dad, Mandip, is the youngest of the three brothers. The oldest is Uncle Malkit, who is about forty-five. He's married to a witch called Pritam and they've got four kids, all older than me. There's Jagtar and Inderjit, the lads, who are both in their late teens, and Rajinder and Gurpreet, who I never see because they are both married to Glaswegians and live in Scotland.

Then there's Uncle Rajbir and Aunt Jagwant. They've got three kids, including Ruby, the youngest, who's a friend as well as a cousin, though I'm not too keen on her older brothers Parmjit and Satnam. They're what I call 'typical bhangra-muffins' – all macho, and thick with it and, to be honest, I don't really speak to them if I can help it.

Ruby is different though, or at least that's what I used to think. She's almost exactly my age. She was born two days before me and we get on really well. Only Ruby has a hard time going out because her parents are so strict. I can't even remember the number of times she's pretended to stay at my parents' just so we can go to parties. My mum sees it as her duty to make sure that Ruby gets to have a life, as long as her mother never finds out. That would mean all-out war in the family, I reckon.

And of course there's my gramps – my dad's father. He's lovely but we don't get to see him that often because he lives at Uncle Malkit's house. On the rare occasions when my uncle allows him to come over, I make him lots of cups of tea and we sit and slag off my aunts. My gramps is amazing because he's more liberal in his outlook than his two eldest sons, which is quite odd in Punjabi families. In the ones I know anyway. Gramps tries to stop the arguments that sometimes brew up, especially between my mum and my aunts, and most of the time he succeeds.

Not that there isn't the odd battle now and then anyway. My dad's brothers run a load of businesses and drive big Mercedes with customized number plates. They look down on my dad because he works in a factory and drives a clapped-out Ford Mondeo. And they think that my brothers and me are wild and lack respect. Not to mention the way they talk about my mum – like she's some kind of madwoman who stole my dad from them. But my dad couldn't care less what they think. My uncles even asked him to join the family business once but he refused. He told us that he was his own man and that he didn't care about fancy things as long as we were happy and we had food to eat, which is really cool, I reckon. It beats being like my uncles anyway: fat, arrogant and obsessed with money.

★ ★ ★

My mum came in about an hour after I got home. She works for a women's community group – the kind of place where battered wives go and stuff – another reason why my dad's family don't like her. I went downstairs and helped her bring the shopping in from the car, all twenty bags of it.

'You expecting guests, Mum?' I asked her.

'That's just what you three eat every week,' she replied.

She was wearing dark jeans, a T-shirt and a sweater, all of which belonged to me. We were almost exactly the same size, although Mum had a bit of extra weight around her hips and belly.

'What about you with your chocolates and wine?' I reminded her. 'Not to mention Homer Simpson and his fat belly . . .'

I was talking about my dad and my mum started to laugh.

'You can't call him that,' she told me when she'd stopped laughing. 'Besides, he's much sexier than Homer . . .'

I shook my head. 'Information I don't need, Mum,' I said.

'I'm only saying that I find your father as attractive now as I did when—'

'*Enough, Mum!* I don't want to hear it,' I joked.

'But he looks so good in his little—' she began.

'*That's* mental abuse! Number for Childline is by the phone,' I told her. 'One call and you're a jailbird.' I grabbed a bag without looking.

'*Watch it!*' shouted my mum, as a twelve pack of eggs fell out and hit the kitchen floor.

'Oh, shit!' I said.

'Idiot child . . . and don't swear – that's my job.'

'I'm sorry,' I replied, pretending to be gutted. It was a stupid way to pack the eggs anyway – on top of a stuffed bag. What did she expect?

My mum shrugged. 'I'll pop out and get some more later,' she said.

I told her I was going to do my homework.

'Er . . . and who's going to clear up the mess you've made, Simran?' she asked.

'You are,' I said, smiling sweetly. 'Because you're the *bestest* mummy in the whole wide world.'

She shook her head. 'That stopped working when you were about six,' she said, handing me a cloth.

I mimicked her under my breath.

My mum grinned. 'What are you – a parrot?' she asked.

'Oh my *God* – you can't call me a parrot!' I replied, pretending to be shocked.

'Just did.'

'At least I can see where Jay gets his cheek from,' I said to her.

'*You'll* get it in a minute,' she replied. 'Clean up . . .'

I told her that she was going grey and that her wrinkles were showing.

David

'**Y**ou got two left feet,' my cousin Parmjit told me, as we sat waiting for the other team to show up. It was a Saturday afternoon and the wind was blowing across the park like a mini hurricane, stabbing at me with its cold fingers.

'Always the same,' I replied, ignoring Parmjit. 'How come not one of the other teams turns up on time?'

'All knobheads,' he told me, sniffing. 'What do you expect, bro?'

Parmjit's tall and skinny with dark, greasy hair, pitted skin and a huge nose that he gets from his mum, my aunt Jagwant. He was wearing a team tracksuit. We both played for an Asian side in a local league, and waiting seemed to be part of each game. It was like every other team in the league couldn't be bothered with watches.

'We might be a player short anyway,' said Parmjit's younger brother, Satnam.

I looked at my other cousin and shook my head. 'Who

is it this week?' I asked, wondering whether I should just go home. Spots of rain began to fall and the sky turned dark grey, leaching away the light.

'Suky Mann,' Satnam told me. 'Fuckin' wedding or some shit . . .'

'But he must have known he had a wedding ages ago,' I said.

Satnam shrugged his broad shoulders. He had a black scarf tied around his head, low on his brow, with long tails that hung down his back. Like he was some Bollywood bad bwoi.

'Don't matter – ain't like we don't go to weddings. Family business comes first . . .'

'So not only am I gonna freeze before the game starts but once it does, I'm gonna end up running around like a fool 'cos we's a player short? Again.'

The rain began to come down more heavily.

'Let's get in the car,' shouted Parmjit.

We followed him to his Audi A3 and got in, as the other team members took shelter too. The rain waited until we were inside before it changed its rhythm and began to pound harder. Parmjit flicked the key around one click and the stereo burst into life, bhangra beats matching the raindrops.

'Turn it down,' I said. 'I'm getting a headache.'

'Stupid white bwoi name *and* he don't like bhangra,' sneered Satnam.

'Shut up, you fat knob,' I replied. I was sick of people telling me my name wasn't right for an Asian. I'd had it all my life and the jokes weren't funny any more.

'You should have a good Punjabi name, son. You

already think you're white anyways,' continued my younger cousin.

'Just hush up,' I told him. 'I can't be doin' wit' your shit today.'

Parmjit turned the music down and turned round to face me. 'So – you still knockin' round with that *kalah*?' he asked, using the Punjabi word for a black man.

'If you mean Dean, then yeah, I am,' I replied, hoping that he wasn't going to launch into one of his rants like he normally did. If he hadn't been my cousin, I wouldn't have had anything to do with him. But family's family and all that.

'Can he play?' said Parmjit.

Satnam laughed. 'In a tree, prob'ly.'

I looked at him and shook my head. 'If you're gonna start cussin' my best mate, I'm gone,' I threatened.

'I'm only havin' a laugh, innit?' replied Satnam, grinning. 'You wanna learn to tek joke.'

I gave him a hard stare. 'Only it ain't a joke – is it?' I said. 'It's what you think. *Twat* . . .'

'Forget you, man. Pussy—'

'Leave it out,' snapped Parmjit, glaring at us both. 'You don't diss family – understand?'

'You do if they're like him,' I said.

'No you *don't*,' Parmjit told me. '*Nothin*' is thicker than blood.'

'Apart from Satnam,' I said.

Satnam called me a few names in Punjabi and then the conversation switched back to the football game.

'There they are,' said Parmjit, nodding in the direction of the park.

'About fuckin' time too,' I said.

'Must be a pub team,' said Satnam. 'Full of white bwoi . . .'

'What's that got to do with anything?' I asked.

'Them white teams are pure racist,' Satnam replied.

'Not all of them,' I argued.

'White bastards,' he snapped, not understanding his own hypocrisy. But then again, he probably couldn't even spell the word.

'You should get your mate to come play for us,' said Parmjit.

'Who – *Dean*?' I asked.

'Yeah . . . if he's any good, that is . . .' he added.

'*Good?* The man is two-footed, fast and he can play anywhere. He's better than anyone we've got playing,' I replied, feeling proud of my mate.

'So bring him down to training,' said Parmjit.

I shrugged. 'He's happy playing for Hillfields – and anyway, why would he want to listen to you lot slag off black people? Don't think so.'

'Ain't like that, is it? We ain't gonna diss him to his *face* – you get me?'

I shook my head at him. 'That makes it OK then,' I said, sarcastically.

'You *know* what I mean,' said Parmjit. 'When we're sayin' that shit – it's just having a laugh, that's all.'

'Yeah,' added Satnam. 'I got 'nuff *kaleh* mates.'

'So how come I ain't seen one of them yet?' I asked.

''Cos after school we all done different things,' replied Parmjit.

Satnam grinned. 'Yeah, they all went to prison and we done all the work.'

I looked at him, wondering whether I'd get away with punching his head in. In the end I just shrugged at them both. 'Ain't nuttin' but racists,' I told them.

'Shut up, you pussy,' said Parmjit, shaking his head at me.

I met up with Dean in town after the football and he asked me how it had gone.

'We drew,' I told him.

'Seen . . .'

'Shit game.'

'You always say that after you've played for them. Why don't you just leave?' he asked me.

'Can't. It's a family thing . . .'

Dean smiled at me. He was wearing faded jeans and low-profile trainers that looked like canoes stuck on the end of his legs.

'If eating shit was a family thing would you still have to do that too?' he joked.

I grinned. 'Prob'ly,' I said.

The rain had worn off and the sun was trying to break through the clouds. We headed into The Shires shopping centre, dodging past the gangs of youths that were milling around, doing nothing much.

'It's like you can't move in here at the weekend,' Dean said, sidestepping an older lad with a frown all over his face and the kind of walk that tells people he thinks he's a bad boy.

'What's his problem?' I said, well after he was out of earshot.

Dean shrugged. 'Altitude,' he suggested.

'You mean attitude?' I corrected.

'That too,' he told me, walking into Debenham's.

'What we goin' in here for?'

'I wanna check out some clothes – seen a wicked jacket in here last week,' said Dean.

We fought our way past the perfume and cosmetics counters and into the menswear section at the back of the ground floor. As we turned into a designer concession I saw the 'jacket' Dean was on about.

'You lyin' git – you ain't here for no jacket,' I said to him.

Dean shrugged and half smiled. In front of us, standing at a till looking bored, was April Brown, a girl from our area, who at eighteen was two years older than us.

'Bwoi – she's one good-looking sister,' said Dean, as though he'd never noticed her before. Never made a fool of himself by following her home. Never sent her expensive flowers anonymously. Or been threatened by her boyfriend.

'So what you gonna do to make yourself look stupid this time?' I asked him.

'Shut up, bro. I'm just checking her out—'

'But you're always checking her out,' I said.

Dean shook his head at me. 'You think that them man who live near the Pyramids in Egypt stop looking at them *ever*? Like they get *used* to them? No way, Jose . . .'

'What the fuck you on about?'

'When there's a wonder of astounding natural beauty in the city where you live – you should go check it out as often as you can,' he explained.

'So basically you're gonna make a twat of yourself every time you see April?' I asked, realizing that he already did.

'One day you'll be asking me how I got her to be *my* girl, bro. Crying yerself to sleep 'cos I've got her in my bed at night.'

'You're livin' in a dream world, mate—'

Just as I spoke, April reached down to pick up something off the floor and we watched in awe as her jeans stretched across her arse, showing its shape to perfection.

Dean turned round. 'I can't look at that,' he told me, looking flustered. 'I'm gonna *pass out* or something. You *see that?*'

I nodded.

'Ain't no finer girl in this city,' he added.

'You need a tissue and a quiet moment?' I asked.

'Don't joke about it, bro,' he told me.

'Come on,' I said. 'I'm hungry — let's grab a McNasty.'

Dean nodded. 'Yeah — I *need* to get out of here . . .'

106 MERE ROAD, LEICESTER – NOVEMBER 1979

The radio in the living room was on when Mandip opened his eyes. He could just about hear The Police singing *Walking on the Moon* as he looked at the clock on the mantelpiece in the bedroom. It was 5.45 a.m. on a cold, grey Saturday morning. The light from the streetlamp outside 106 Mere Road filtered orange through the dusty curtains. Mandip groaned and put his head back under the blankets.

Five minutes later he tried to get up again, looking across the room to the two other single beds, pushed together in the corner, where his older brothers slept. But they had already left for work and he realized that his dad would be up to get him if he didn't move. He looked for his shoes, slipping them on and going downstairs. When he walked into the living room, his dad was already shaved, dressed and ready to go.

'Hurry up, Mandip!' Gulbir Singh Gill told his son in Punjabi.

'But it's cold,' replied the nine-year-old.

'Stop being such a girl,' added Gulbir.

'Where's Mum?' asked Mandip.

His dad smiled and shook his head. 'In the kitchen making tea and paratha,' he replied.

Mandip's shoes made a *clop, clop, clop* noise on the linoleum floor as he crossed the room to go and see his mum but his dad called him back.

'Did you bring the bucket down?' he asked.

Mandip turned up his nose and shook his head.

'Go and get it then – it's not going to empty itself.'

The bucket his dad was talking about acted as a toilet overnight, when no one could be bothered to go to the outdoor lavatory in the back yard to relieve themselves. Of all the jobs that Mandip hated, he hated this one the worst. The alkaline stink made his eyes sting and his throat tighten but he did it anyway, careful not to let the foul liquid slop about too much and wet his pyjamas. In the back yard he poured the contents down the drain and left the bucket in a corner. He turned quickly back into the house, shivering from the cold, ready for a cup of tea.

Mandip took in the familiar morning smell of spiced tea and buttered paratha, washed his hands and then watched his mum as she cooked.

'You better take your big coat today,' she told him, as he heard the new song by a band called Madness filter in from the living room. It was the most popular song at his school and he smiled as he remembered his best friend Mikey humming it in class, winding up Wayne King, a white boy in the same class, who had told them that Madness were an NF band.

'No!' Mikey had replied. 'They're a ska band – me dad tol' me—'

'No they ain't,' added Wayne. 'They ain't no darkies . . .'

'But it's black people's music,' Mikey had told Wayne.

Later on, in the playground, Mandip had asked Mikey if he could listen to black people's music too.

'Yeah!' Mikey had told him. 'You an' me is both black . . .'

'But I'm brown,' Mandip had said.

'So? My *dad* says that the NF hate us all anyway, so we're all black – that's what *my* dad says.'

Mandip grinned as he remembered smiling at what his best friend had said. The sudden sharp pain in his ear brought him back to the present.

'Are you listening?' his mum asked him.

'Yes . . .'

'Good – it's going to snow today so take your hat and gloves too – and take your dad his tea.'

In the living room twenty minutes later, after his youngest son had washed and dressed, Gulbir Singh listened to the news reports on his radio. Leicester City were playing at home, according to the man on the radio, and Gulbir swore.

'What's up, Dad?' asked his youngest son.

'Nothing,' lied Gulbir, even though he knew that every home game brought trouble for all the non-white traders on Leicester market. For a moment he considered taking the day off but the thought lasted only just long enough for him to swear at *it* too.

'Come on!' he told Mandip. 'Time to go . . .'

Mandip ran into the kitchen and hugged his mum. She handed him a package of paratha wrapped in brown paper, and then followed him out onto the street, where it was still dark. Gulbir Singh's van chugged and gurgled and spat out white smoke as it warmed up. From down the street he heard someone hail his dad.

'Yes – I, Missa Singh!'

'OK,' he heard his dad reply in his heavily accented English.

'Everyt'ing irie?' asked the tall black man, his eyes half closed and a can of Skol 45 in his hands.

'Rass class, Winston . . .' replied Gulbir, climbing into the van.

'Niceness . . .' agreed Winston, before ruffling Mandip's hair. 'Easy, likkle Missa Singh . . .'

Mandip blushed and climbed in beside his dad as the black man walked on down to his own door. He turned to his dad.

'Why is that man drunk so early?' he asked.

Gulbir smiled. 'He's just coming home from a party,' he explained, unsure whether his youngest would understand.

'Must have been an early party,' replied a confused Mandip.

Gulbir chuckled to himself. 'Or a very late one,' he said, sliding the door shut and letting off the handbrake. When his dad turned on the radio Mandip heard his favourite song, 'OK Fred' by Errol Dunkley, and sang along.

SIMRAN

'So, at least walk back with me,' pleaded Tyrone. I watched his eyes sparkle and nodded. 'All right then – but it doesn't mean anything . . .' I insisted.

'Yeah – it does.' He grinned. 'It means that you're warming up, sister.'

'Whatever . . .' I replied, sounding like an annoying American teenager in a Hollywood movie.

It was Monday lunchtime and I had walked down to the row of shops by our school. I'd been buying a new notepad in the newsagent's when Tyrone walked in with two of his mates. We'd stood and chatted for about half an hour and now we were heading back. Tyrone walked in a confident way, like he was completely sure of himself, which I kind of liked. His friends had disappeared and I asked him if he had told them to leave again.

'Yeah, I did,' he told me.

'Why?' I asked.

''Cos I wanted to be alone with you . . . same as last time,' he admitted.

'I'm not worth it,' I said. 'I'm not looking for a boyfriend.'

'Not yet,' he replied. 'But when you are – I'm first in line . . .'

I smiled at him for his arrogance. It was a confident, appealing arrogance. 'And what makes you think that?' I asked.

'Perseverance. I'm the one that's doing all the running . . .'

'But that doesn't guarantee you first place,' I teased.

'So what does?'

'Oh, I don't know,' I joked. 'Flowers, chocolates, a nice *diamond*?'

He shook his head. 'Might be out of my reach – that diamond . . .'

'Well, there you go then,' I said.

'You're just playin', sister.'

'Maybe I am,' I replied. 'But not with you . . .'

'*Nah!* How can someone so pretty be so tough?' he asked me.

I blushed and looked away, despite the fact that it felt great to be called pretty. I'd never thought of myself as pretty. I knew that I wasn't ugly but I didn't like my nose and my eyes were too big. And my hair had this strange wave in it that I couldn't get rid of no matter how hard I tried. And even though people called my shape voluptuous, I didn't see it as a compliment. As far as I could see my bum was too big. But Tyrone *was* winning brownie points. Just not enough to get him what he wanted.

'I'm actually a complete bitch,' I told him. 'I can kill men with one stare.'

'I used to know this girl once . . .' began Tyrone.

My heart sank for a split second. I thought he was going to tell me about an ex-girlfriend and I felt jealous. Weirdo girl or what?

'Could knock man out with one whiff of her armpit,' he finished.

Relieved, I began to grin. 'That's nasty,' I said.

He laughed. 'Yeah – she was.'

'That's a bit mean,' I said.

Tyrone looked at me to see if I was joking so I put on a stern face. 'I was only kidding,' he said quickly, thinking that he was going to have to dig himself out of a hole. I waited a few moments before grinning again.

'Gotcha!' I said, as we turned down the road that led to my school.

'You're too harsh, sister,' he said.

'I gotta go, anyway,' I replied, ignoring him.

'Just like that?' he asked. 'Not even a peck on the cheek for all the joke I've been runnin' since we started walking back?' He shook his head as though he was gutted.

'Here,' I said, digging in my bag for a mouldy old half-eaten Mars bar that I knew was there, and holding it out for him, 'you can have this as a token of my esteem . . .'

He took the chocolate and looked at it as though it was some strange new species of animal. 'You know what?' he said. 'I think I'll leave it.'

'You can't now,' I told him. 'You have to eat it if you want to talk to me again . . .'

I was only joking but Tyrone's eyes sparkled and

a beautiful grin spread across his face. He was so cute.

'OK – here's the deal, sister,' he told me. 'I'll eat this . . . this t'ing – whatever it is – but you have to give me your digits—'

'My what?'

'Yer digits, sister – for your phone . . .' he explained.

'Oh – you want my phone number?'

'Yeah – that's what I just said.'

'No you didn't.' I grinned. 'You were on about my digits . . .'

'I know, but—'

'And we've not known each other long enough for me to just get my digits out – what sort of girl do you think I am?'

'But I was on about—' he began, until he saw me smile. 'Piss-taker . . .'

'Won't get my number by calling me names, will you?' I pointed out.

Tyrone looked at the stale chocolate bar. 'So we got a deal or what?' he asked.

I thought about it for a moment. If he was willing to eat a rank old chocolate bar just to get my number then he deserved to have it. I nodded. 'Deal.'

Tyrone looked at me, smiled and then unpicked the wrapper from the chocolate. It took a while because it was firmly stuck, but eventually he had a golfball-sized dollop of melted and re-formed Mars bar with bits of fluff on it in his hand. He looked at me again and then shoved it in his mouth, chewing it up quickly and swallowing hard.

'I can't believe you just ate that,' I said, beginning to laugh.

He finished swallowing and shrugged. ''S only chocolate — what's the worst that could happen?' he asked.

'But it's been in my bag since last year,' I told him, lying through my teeth. It was only about three months old. Although that was bad enough, I suppose.

For a moment Tyrone began to look a bit green, but then he remembered the deal and grinned. 'Phone number,' he reminded me.

I got my phone out and saw the time. 'Shit! I'm late . . .'

'Still need them digits,' he insisted.

I shouted out my number as I ran off towards school, feeling like I was on top of the world, not even making sure that he'd heard it right. Though, deep down inside, I wanted him to have it more and more. I was getting hooked and I needed to talk to Lisa to find out what she thought about it all.

We spoke after school but Lisa was in a hurry to get home and didn't really listen, not that I minded. Instead we said goodbye at my drive and I decided to spend some quality time with my books. I had a heap of work to do, but when I actually sat at my desk I couldn't concentrate at all. All I could think about was Tyrone and whether I would be playing with fire if I went out with him. In the end I decided to research the subject with my parents, only not directly. I planned to test their attitudes by asking sly questions when they were off-guard. I spent the rest of the evening on the Net, instant messaging my cousin Ruby and another friend, Paula, Dean's sister, waiting and hoping for my mobile to buzz and tell me that I had a message. I didn't let on about Tyrone to either of them, although I thought about speaking to Paula about the whole black/Asian thing. In the end though I chickened out, deciding to leave it for another time.

SIMRAN

Lisa sat down on my bed and put the cup of tea that I'd made for her on my bedside table. I looked at her and wished that my legs were as long as hers. She was wearing blue, boot-cut jeans with a tight white T-shirt; and K-Swiss with a reversible red tongue. Her light brown hair was piled on top of her head, which did two things: it made her slim, athletic figure and perfectly symmetrical face look even better and me much more envious.

'*How many texts?*' she asked me for the fourth time.

'Ten,' I repeated.

'*Ten?*'

'Yeah . . . that's what I said – about *fifty* times . . .'

She grinned at me. 'There's no need to *exaggerate* now, is there?' she joked.

'Well – you know what I mean. I only *gave* him my number yesterday . . .'

'Well, he *is* a boy,' Lisa reminded me.

'*And?*'

'They don't have control over those urges the way we do. Everything has to be today. What do you think wanking's all about?'

I shook my head. Trust Lisa to lower the tone – the dirty cow.

'He's just interested, that's all,' I told her.

'You're telling *me*. So, are you gonna go out with him?'

I shook my head again. 'Don't think so,' I admitted. 'He's really fit and all that but I'm not sure . . .'

'Why not?' she asked.

I wondered how to tell her what was on my mind. In a way that wouldn't make me out to be racist or anything.

'Erm . . . it's just that . . .' I began.

'That he's fit, funny and *wants* to go out with you? Yeah, I can see how that is a major problem, Simmy.'

'I know all that,' I sighed. 'It's just that I can't, I don't think—'

'Speak English, you witch.'

I took a sip of tea and tried to think of a clever way of saying what I wanted to say. But nothing clever sprang to mind and in the end I decided to be honest.

'It's because he's black,' I admitted, instantly feeling ashamed of myself. Not because I was bothered by his skin colour; because I was worried what my family might say about it – my extended family.

Lisa gave me a funny look and then looked away for a second. Long enough to tell me that she wasn't happy with what I'd just said.

'I'm not a racist,' I insisted. 'Honestly.'

'But you just said that you won't see him 'cos he's black,' she pointed out. 'Sounds kind of dubious to me . . .'

'It's not about *me*,' I told her.

'What is it about then?' she asked.

'My family . . .'

'But your dad is best mates with a black man,' she reminded me.

She was right too. My dad's best friend was a man called Michael Ricketts – Uncle Mikey. Our families were so close that my brother's best mate was Uncle Mikey's son Dean, and his daughter Paula, who was older than me, was a good friend of mine. I had grown up with Dean and Paula. We went round for dinner all the time, as a family, or they came to us. And my mum and Aunty Carleen often went out together. But I wasn't talking about my parents and I told Lisa so.

'So who *are* you on about, you weirdo?' she asked.

'The rest of them – uncles, aunts, cousins . . .'

She looked at me like I was mad. 'But what do they matter – it's not like they're proper family, are they?' she said.

'They *are* in my parents' culture . . .'

'And what – they're all racists so you have to be one too?' she asked.

'It's not *like* that,' I protested. 'I'm not like them. It's just that there's this Asian thing—'

'Being racist?'

'No . . . not just that. It's like this inbuilt thing that some Asians have . . .' I tried to explain.

'*Just because Tyrone's black?*' She shook her head in disbelief.

37

I shrugged and tried desperately to think of that clever way of explaining but it still didn't come to me.

'It's the same with different religions too,' I began. 'Muslims go out with Muslims, Sikhs with Sikhs – that kind of thing.'

Lisa raised an eyebrow. 'But what about Geeta – that girl from Year Eleven? She's a Hindu and she was seeing a Muslim lad—'

'*Yeah* – and what happened to *her*?' I asked.

'I dunno – what *did* happen?' replied Lisa.

'Her old man found out and her brothers beat up her boyfriend.'

Lisa tried to grin and lighten the mood. 'OK then – maybe that wasn't the *best* example in the world, but—'

I shook my head and cut her off. 'Most of my family would go mad if I went out with Tyrone – it's just something that doesn't happen very much.'

'I still don't get it,' Lisa told me. 'He's just a boyfriend. It ain't like you're going to marry the idiot . . .'

'My uncles would see it as dishonourable and give my parents a load of shit about it,' I said.

'*So?*'

'So – it's not worth the grief,' I added.

'Man – you Asians are weird,' she half joked.

'Oh shut up, BNP girl.'

'Well, what do you expect me to say? If a *white* person said what you've just said, they'd get *slated* and you know it,' she pointed out.

'I know. I'm not saying that I think like my uncles but . . .'

Lisa shook her head again. 'But nothing, Simmy. The minute you start excusing racism—'

'*I'm not racist!*' I snapped.

'*Whoa, Nelly!* No need to get angry.'

I looked at her and shrugged. 'Sorry . . .'

'You should be . . .'

'*Lisa!*'

'*Well* – I'm still a bit shocked. If you want to go out on a date with Tyrone, you should. Forget what your extended family think. *Who cares?*' she said.

'I know you're right but I just can't stop thinking about what they would say,' I admitted.

'I don't get it. I wouldn't think twice about going out with someone who was a different colour to me if I liked them. And my parents wouldn't care either.'

I sighed. 'Oh, I don't know what to do,' I told her.

I spoke to Priti, a friend from school, later that evening, thinking that she would say the same things Lisa had. But I was in for a shock. I was sitting on my bed, looking at the blank screen on my PC as I spoke to her.

'Don't do it,' she said.

'Huh?'

'Don't do it.'

'But I thought that you'd—'

'Simran, don't be so naïve – you know how things work . . .'

'Yeah, I do,' I agreed. 'But why should I listen to what people say – surely if I like him and I want to go out with him, I can?'

'All you'll get is mountains of grief from other Asian

people – especially lads – and all for some stupid fling that probably won't last anyway.'

'You don't know that,' I said.

'Yes I do. My friend's cousin got pregnant by a black lad and she was kicked out of the house.'

'Yeah, but my parents ain't like that,' I told her.

'You're definitely being naïve, Simmy. I told you – it's just not worth the grief. And believe me – you'll get shit – loads of it.'

'But I really like him,' I said.

'So? There's plenty of other lads about . . .'

'But he's not other lads,' I protested.

'Look – I'm not bein' funny but black/Asian things don't work . . . it's not racism – it's just . . .'

We went on like that for another twenty minutes and then I got another text from Tyrone. I rang off and looked at it, smiling as I read. I didn't stop thinking about it all evening, even as I was trying to go to sleep. I really wanted to go out with Tyrone, at least for one date, but something was holding me back. I thought about asking my mum but realized that my original idea was the best way forward. I would test the water first.

DAVID

My dad eyed me with suspicion.

'So you weren't part of that fight at all then?' he asked.

I shook my head. 'I didn't know anything about it until you rang to find out where I was,' I replied.

'Oh yeah,' he remembered. 'You told me that you and Dean were bunkin' off . . .'

I shrugged. 'I was hopin' that you'd forget about that,' I said.

'Fat chance.'

I grinned at him as he shifted in his favourite chair, holding tightly onto his bottle of Becks. The bottle sat on his belly, which looked as though it had been stuck on as an extra. The rest of him was all long and skinny.

'Well, you *is* fat so there's a bit of a chance—'

'You cheeky little shit – I should tan your backside for skipping school.'

'We weren't really bunking off – it was a free period,' I told him, hoping that he'd fall for it.

'Wass one of them then? Di'n't have them in my day.'

'Yeah, and you didn't have computers or mobiles – or shoes,' I said, taking the piss.

'Or big mouths that could get stuffed with my socks,' he threatened.

'Sorry, Homer . . .'

'I should tell Mikey about it too,' he told me – Mikey was Dean's dad – his best mate.

'Nah! You can't do that – that's grassin'.'

'You gotta go to school, David – them's the rules, boy.'

'But—'

'But nothing. You think me and Mikey sweat in that shithole factory all week just to watch our kids fuck up like we did?'

I was ready with a smart reply but I wasn't expecting him to say what he did. Not the swearing – he swore all the time. More the stuff about messing up and not wanting me to do the same. I'd always thought that he was happy with his life and I wanted to know if I was wrong. So I asked him.

'It's just an expression,' he told me. 'I meant that we want the best for our kids and that means getting an education – doing the stuff we never did.'

I looked at him, puzzled. 'Like what?' I asked.

'University and travel and learning because you *want* to; not because some old git in a suit is telling you to.'

'But you and Mum are always travelling,' I reminded him.

'Not just holidays, David – I'm talking about discovering things and stuff . . .'

And with that he went off on one, talking about the great things that he wanted to see before he died, like the big rock in the middle of Australia, which I told him was called Uluru, and the statues on Easter Island. I listened to him for a bit, got him two more beers and then went to call Dean to see if he fancied going out for a bit. When I went back into the living room with my jacket, my old man was snoring.

Dean told me to meet him down on Evington Road, by a fried chicken shop, and when I got there he was scoffing a portion of hot wings, getting the grease all over his face.

'Yussusus!' he mumbled through a mouthful of food.

'Easy . . .'

He swallowed his mouthful and grinned at me. 'My man knows how to make chicken,' he told me. 'Hot!'

'Yeah, he knows how to make money too,' I replied. 'He's opened about ten shops in a year or summat.'

'Can't argue with that if the food is good,' Dean said.

'What we doin' anyway?' I asked him.

He shrugged. 'How 'bout we go check out the community centre?' he suggested.

'Yeah – and I can kick yer ass at table tennis again,' I said.

'Res' yuhself! That was a lucky win, bro.'

'Yeah – if you say so.'

I heard an engine roar and turned to see a Subaru Impreza burn up the road and jump a red light.

'Knobs . . .' said Dean, screwing up the empty box of chicken and throwing it in the general direction of a bin. The box bounced off, landing in the road, next to the wheel of a 3 Series BMW.

'Three points!' he said, opening a freshen-up tissue and wiping his hands.

I looked at my mate and shook my head. 'Messy shit . . .'

Dean shrugged and set off for the community centre, the tissue following the flight path of the box and ending up next to it.

The community centre was pretty empty apart from a couple of groups of lads and three girls who were always there. The table tennis table was free and we picked up the paddles, found a ball that wasn't too knackered and started to play. Only I wasn't really paying attention to the ball. I noticed that some of the youths were from our school. One of the group, Pally, was an old friend of mine from infant school, and I told Dean that I was going to talk to him. Dean shrugged and went over to the girls, who were sitting near a coffee machine, chatting.

'Easy, Pally,' I said. He was wearing really tight blue jeans and massive Nike Shox with a hooded top and stood about an inch shorter than me – five foot eight, maybe.

'David – wass up, bro?' he replied, extending a fist for me to touch.

'Usual – what happened with that fight?'

'The one up by school?' he asked.

I wondered which other fights he'd been in and said yes.

'Been comin' a while, that one,' he told me. 'Too much shit goin' on with that Rajinder Mann and them black lads from City . . .'

'What kind of shit?' I asked.

'He got into it with some lad from City. All came from that,' replied Pally.

'Just one argument?'

Pally shook his head. 'Nah – there was a few things. One of them *kaleh* tried it on with Raji's cousin's sister and Raji got upset . . .'

'Over a bit of flirtin'?'

Pally gave me a funny look, like I'd asked him to show me his arse or something. 'Can't have that,' he said. 'Raji di'n't want no *kalah* fuckin' wid his family . . .'

'So Raji started it just 'cos the bloke was black?' I asked, ignoring Pally's casual racism. He wasn't the only Asian lad who was like that and I couldn't fight them all. At least not right then.

'Prob'ly . . .' replied Pally.

'The papers said it was purely racial . . .'

Pally shrugged. 'It was Desi Posse versus the rest, bro. Them papers just chat shit anyway. I know for a *fact* there was Asian lads from City wit' dem *kaleh*.'

I shook my head. 'Sounds messed up to me,' I said.

'Too right, bro. And there's more comin' – believe me. Raji and two other lads got kicked out of school. One of 'em is goin' down for stabbin' that teacher—'

'Who?' I asked.

'Raji's cousin. Divy Mann . . .'

'The man with the streak in his hair?'

'The same one, bro.'

I looked over at Dean, who was busy chatting up one of the girls.

'You best watch it an' all,' Pally told me.

I gave him a funny look. 'What's it gotta do with me?' I asked.

'It's comin' like an "us and dem" t'ing — you get me?'

I shook my head and said no.

'Yer man there — Dean. Now I ain't got nuttin' against him — he's OK with me; but the Desi are goin' after that other gang an' if they see you with a nex' *kalah*, they might get vex an' that . . .'

'Not my problem,' I told him. 'They mess with Dean — they got me to deal with too.'

Pally nodded as though I'd explained something really complicated to him. 'I'm just sayin', that's all,' he said. 'Like I said — Dean is fine with me . . .'

I gave him another funny look. '*But* . . . ?'

'But if it do come down to "us and dem" I'm with "us" . . .' he said.

I left it at that and went over to Dean. He was keying the girl's number into his phone.

'Come on, bro — let's do one,' I said.

'Just comin',' Dean replied, before speaking to the girl, whose name was Leanne. 'I'll call you,' he told her.

'You better, Dean — that's the third time I've given you my number. Ain't gonna *be* a nex' time . . .'

'No worries,' he said, grinning.

Then he turned and followed me outside, where I told him what I'd learned from Pally. The wind had picked up and as we walked back home, Dean pulled his hood over his head and tightened it.

'Does that bother you?' he asked me.

'What?'

'That whole Asian versus black bullshit t'ing?'

I shook my head. 'I ain't into that,' I told him, although he already knew that.

'And it don't bother me neither,' he said. 'So fuck them, bwoi . . .'

'You're right,' I said.

'If they wanna mash themselves up 'cos one a dem Asian and the other one black – let 'em. Best we just stay well clear, you get me?'

'True.'

'Unless they wanna tes',' he said with a smile.

'And then what?' I asked, although this time it was me who already knew the answer.

'Then we watch each other's back – same as always, bro . . .'

I nodded and pulled up my own hood, as the wind started to howl like a hungry wolf all around us.

SUKY MANN AND
SATNAM GILL

Satnam watched his cousin David run after the football before turning to Suky.

'He's fast, man,' he said.

'Yeah – though I should still be playin',' Suky replied, picking at the grass they were sitting on.

'You would have been if you'd turned up for practice,' Satnam pointed out.

'Couldn't be done, bro. I was round my cousin Divy's house – he's gettin' sent down . . .'

Satnam looked at Suky and raised an eyebrow. 'For what?' he asked.

'Some shit at school – got into it with a load of lads from a nex' school.'

Satnam nodded his head. 'He the one that stabbed that teacher?' he asked.

Suky nodded. 'Yeah, but it weren't his fault.

They were fightin' a load of *kaleh* when it happened.'

'I heard about it,' replied Satnam. 'My bro,' he continued, nodding in David's direction, 'he goes there an' all.'

'He's the one that knocks around with that big nigger, in't he?' asked Suky, before spitting.

'Yeah – best mate or summat,' admitted Satnam.

'He wants to be careful. Them *kaleh* look after their own when it comes down to it, you get me?'

'We told him that 'nuff times,' replied Satnam.

'There's gonna be more trouble. My other cousin, Raji, got kicked out of school too and that man is nuts.'

Satnam heard a shout go up and turned his attention back to the game. He saw his brother Parmjit arguing with some white lad, before the referee calmed them down and awarded a free kick in the white lad's favour.

'*Bias!*' he shouted, as the kick was taken. 'See how you help yer own kind, ref!'

'Cheatin' bastard,' added Suky, agreeing with his team mate, even though he hadn't seen the incident.

They watched the game for a few more minutes before Suky spoke again.

'Anyways, like I said before – it's gonna kick off with them black lads and my cousin, and when that happens you wanna make sure David backs his own side.'

'Anyone touches my family . . .' warned Satnam.

'I'm just sayin' – that's all,' replied Suky. 'Ain't right for him to be takin' their side.'

Satnam nodded. 'I'll have a word, but he's still family . . .'

'When it comes down to Desi versus the rest, bro, we's all family,' said Suky.

'Can't argue with that,' said Satnam, nodding again. 'I'll speak to him.'

SIMRAN

I spent the whole of the following week trying to ignore Tyrone's text messages but he wouldn't take no for an answer, and when I made the mistake of replying, it just made him more eager. Luckily I didn't see him at all during the week because I'm not sure I would have been able to fool him face to face. I would have been saying no when everything about my expression and body language would have been saying yes. And I'm sure he would have seen straight through it all. Or pretended to at least.

Lisa just laughed at me every time Tyrone's name came up. And by the time we were heading into town on the bus the following Saturday, she was urging me to call him.

'*Go on!*' she insisted, as the bus hit a pothole.

'They should sort the bloody roads out – I think I've got whiplash,' I said.

'Don't ignore me, you cow – just call the poor lad and

put him out of his misery. What you're doing is cruel,' she added.

'Cruel?'

'Yeah – like tying a tortoise to a treadmill and turning up the speed.'

I gave her a look that told her I thought she was mad. 'A *tortoise* – to a *treadmill*?' I asked, grinning.

'Oh – you *know* what I mean,' said Lisa.

'Er . . . no, actually, I don't think that I do.'

'*Oooh* – check out Miss Fancy Knickers and her perfect English!'

'You *what*?'

Lisa grinned at me. 'Just ask the boy out,' she said, completing a circle back to where she had started, but leaving me confused, and *still* wondering why anyone would do that to a tortoise and what was so fancy about my accent.

'You're just bloody strange . . .' I told her.

'Yep!'

A couple of lads got on the bus and Lisa swore.

'What's up?' I asked.

'See that tall one?' she whispered.

'Yeah?' I whispered back.

'Got off with him.'

'So what?' I asked.

'Threw up on him at a party.'

'*And . . . ?*'

'We were kissing, and he had his hands everywhere and I was really drunk,' she whispered. 'Anyway, he got his *thing* out and when I saw it I threw up all down him.'

'*Lisa!*' I shouted. The dirty cow.

'*Sssshhh!*'

The tall lad looked over his shoulder at us, shook his head and then returned to his conversation.

'*See?*' I told her. 'Like he even gives a shit.'

'But—' she began.

'But *nothing*, young lady. I think it's time you told me some more about what you get up to when I'm not around,' I said.

'You *were* there – it was that party for Joss – the weirdo girl with the big hooters and the massive house—'

'Big *hooters?*' I asked, disgusted.

'Yeah – you know – *breasts* . . . ?' said Lisa, like she was explaining to a very stupid child.

'I know what you meant . . . it's just you sounded like some lad. *Hooters* is a horrible word,' I complained.

'Oh, shut up – that's what my dad calls them and I kind of like the word. It's better than tits.'

'Strange,' I replied. 'You. Very. Strange.'

'Anyways – we were at this party, you and me—'

'I,' I corrected.

'Huh?'

'You and I were at this party,' I continued.

'Exactly what I said, you and me was at this party—'

'But—' I began.

'Oh shut up, you slag, and listen,' snapped Lisa.

'*I'm* the slag? Who threw up when she saw tall boy's joystick?' I asked.

'Joystick? *Joystick?*'

'Er . . .' I began, realizing that it was a silly way to describe a willy.

'And you think *hooters* is a silly word – man, you're tapped,' Lisa said.

'Just get on with the story, will you? *Jesus*, we'll be in town before you've finished.' I looked out of the window as I spoke, realizing that we were in town already.

She told me the rest of it as we got off the bus and walked down towards the clock tower, in a really loud voice so that people could hear what she was on about.

I didn't see Tyrone in town either, which was a bit strange because he was normally knocking around in The Shires shopping centre with his mates. But I didn't think too much of it, especially when later he sent me three texts within five minutes, begging me to go out with him and telling me that if I didn't he would fail at school because he couldn't concentrate on his work. His descent into unemployment, drug abuse and even prostitution would then be my fault, he said. I laughed to myself as I stood in the kitchen at home, watching my mum make a curry.

'What you laughing at?' she asked me.

'Oh nothing – just this girl I know,' I said slyly. 'She's got this lad on her case but she doesn't know whether she should go out with him or not.'

My mum started to chop up an onion, so quickly that I thought she would cut off a finger by mistake. She was good with a knife, she always said, which was one of the reasons why my dad was nice to her. She didn't offer a reply to what I'd just said though, so I pushed it some more.

'The lad is black and she's Punjabi,' I added, hoping to get her attention. I did.

She looked at me and shrugged. 'That could be a sticking point,' she said.

'*Why?*' I asked, adding layers to my sly-cake. Bit by bit.

'Well – depends on what her parents are like . . .' she told me.

'You mean – if they're prejudiced?'

'Yeah, that too – but mainly if they're like a traditional Punjabi family.'

She wiped the blade of the knife on a piece of kitchen towel and started to chop up some garlic too.

'How'd you mean?' I asked. Sly-cake was now a good few tiers and growing.

'A lot of Punjabis want their kids to marry their own kind . . . it's not exactly racist – just one of those things.'

'So black boys are out of bounds then?'

She shook her head. 'Not for everyone – I told you: depends on the family. But it would cause problems, I reckon.'

I frowned. It wasn't the answer I'd been hoping for. I'd been hoping that she would tell me something similar to what Lisa had said about not worrying about race and all that rubbish. To tell you the truth, I was a bit shocked because my mum is normally very liberal. She must have read my mind because she tried to explain herself.

'I mean,' she said, 'I think that people should forget about the whole race and culture thing. But that's quite a naïve attitude because differences between races still cause problems.'

'But—' I began, only for my mum to cut me off.

'Look at the grief me and your dad got – and *we're*

both Punjabi. If I had chosen to marry a black man, the reaction would have been ten times worse.'

'That doesn't make it right,' I pointed out.

'Of course it doesn't, Simmy, but life doesn't always work out fairly,' she told me, as a piece of ginger found itself being chopped to bits by her demonic knife hand.

'So if *Ruby* went out with a black lad – that would cause shit?' I asked, icing my cake.

'*Ruby?*' My mum shook her head and smiled. 'Her parents don't want her seeing *any* boy. Can you imagine what they'd say?'

'But if she did – would you and Dad hate her for it?'

My mum gave me a quizzing look. 'Is there something you're trying to tell me in amongst all these questions?' she asked.

I felt my face going red. 'No . . . nothing like that,' I lied. 'I'm just *asking*, that's all – because of this girl at school.'

'Not Ruby?'

'No – someone else,' I replied.

'Oh, right,' she said. 'No – we wouldn't hate her for it. But some members of her family might.'

I thought back to what Lisa had said about not caring what my extended family might think.

'Yeah,' I said, 'but that extended family thing is all rubbish, isn't it?'

My mum smiled. 'Yes and no,' she said, throwing the onions into a large pan. 'Put it this way – it would cause some grief in our family – especially with your uncles.'

'So what advice would you give this girl at my school

then?' I asked, realizing that I needed to stop asking questions before my mum became suspicious.

'Proceed with caution,' she said.

'Shall I cut up the chicken for you?' I asked her immediately, hoping to change the subject.

My mum eyed me with that look that mums have. Half suspicion, half bemusement. She nodded. 'Yeah – and then maybe we can discuss another moral issue – seeing as this one is obviously finished.'

I grinned at her. 'We could discuss the way that women find weight difficult to shift after their third child,' I offered.

My mum held up the knife. She didn't say anything. She just held it in front of me and made a couple of quick slashes through the air.

'I'll just get that chicken,' I said, hurrying to the fridge.

SIMRAN

The following day I was in Asda with my dad, doing the shopping, when I saw an Asian girl with a black guy and a baby. I looked at them as they walked past me in the cooked meats aisle, catching the girl's eye. She gave me the once over, smiled and walked on. I looked for my dad, who was busy comparing the price of normal bacon to the speciality stuff.

'Six slices for *that much*?' he said. I don't know who he was talking to because I was standing about three metres away from him. I walked over and looked at the packet of bacon rashers.

'Get the cheap ones then,' I told him.

'Yeah – but they're not honey-blossom *smoked*, are they?' he said, expecting me to know what he was on about.

'Did you see that couple?' I asked him, ignoring the great bacon debate.

He shook his head and for a split second I thought he'd been listening to me.

'The cheaper stuff is all thin and I *bet* it shrinks in the pan. This posh stuff is thick cut – the way bacon used to be when I was a lad. We used to get it from the butcher on St Saviour's Road—'

'*Dad . . .*'

He looked at me, then at the packet of bacon in his hand. 'Best get the cheaper stuff – your mum'll kill me otherwise,' he told me.

'*I'll* kill you in a minute . . . Did you *see* that couple?'

He looked round but they had moved on down the next aisle.

'What couple?' he asked, putting the posh bacon back and grabbing the packs of normal stuff.

'Oh, you're useless sometimes. There was an Asian girl with a black guy,' I explained.

'So . . . ?' He moved on to the fridge that held the cooked meats.

'So – that's quite rare, isn't it?' I said.

He shrugged. 'Probably – does Jay like ham or chicken?' he replied.

'*Dad!*'

'What's the big deal? They're a couple – so what?'

I looked at him, realizing that I was being far too obvious. 'I just wondered whether they get shit from people – other Asian people.'

'Maybe they do,' he replied, grabbing a load of chicken slices.

'Get the honey-roasted ones,' I told him, pointing to Jay's favourites.

'Huh?'

'The honey-roasted – Jay doesn't eat any of the others.'

He swapped the packets over and pushed the trolley up to me. 'Why the interest?' he asked me.

'Just wondered – that's all,' I replied, deciding to push my investigation to the edge. 'There's this girl at school, and this black guy keeps asking her out but she won't go out with him because of what her parents might think . . .'

'Oh – right,' my dad said.

'What do *you* think about it?' I pressed.

'My best friend in the whole world is black so what do you think I'm gonna say?' he asked me.

'Oh, right. So you don't think it's a big thing?'

'I didn't *say* that,' he told me, ushering me into the next aisle, where the couple in question were looking at the milk.

'So you *do* think it's a problem . . .'

'For some people,' he said, coming to a stop and looking right at me.

'Like Uncle Rajbir . . . if, for example, Ruby went out with a black guy . . . ?' I asked, really pushing it.

'He'd probably kill them both,' said my dad, without a hint of humour. 'Why – you're not telling me that it's Ruby, are you?'

I shook my head. '*No!* She doesn't go out with boys – period.'

'Because that would cause some serious trouble,' he pointed out.

'But doesn't that *bother* you – the fact that your family is so racist?'

He shrugged. 'Lots of things my brothers think bother me. I just don't care.'

'So you don't mind seeing Asian and black couples then?' I said, lowering my voice as the couple I was on about walked past.

'Not at all. It's none of my business,' he said. 'And look how cute that kid is – he's got as much right to be alive as anyone else.'

I wanted to ask him how he'd feel if it *was* his business. If it was *his* daughter. But his reply told me all I needed to know, or so I thought. Things didn't pan out that way though. Not exactly.

That evening I replied to a couple of Tyrone's messages, cheeky, flirtatious replies that didn't give too much away. Each time I sent a reply, he sent one back within a minute, and after the first two I decided to play a game with him and stop replying. But he just sent me loads more messages that made me giggle to myself. The silly boy. In the end I sent another text, telling him that I would call him soon, but only if he stopped clogging my inbox with his pleas. He sent me a two-word reply: CAN'T WAIT.

I did some homework, sent Paula and Ruby a load of messages on instant messenger and then got really bored. In the end, wanting to tell Lisa how my parents had replied to my sly and not-so-sly questions, I called and asked her what she was up to.

'Not a lot,' she told me. 'Sitting here, trying to do this science project . . .'

'You want some help?' I asked, hoping she'd ask me to come round. She did.

'But I don't need your help. I'll do the project myself.'

'I'll be there in a few,' I said, ringing off.

I went into the bathroom and put my hair up on top of my head before going downstairs. My parents were in the living room, watching rubbish Sunday evening television.

'I'm popping over to Lisa's,' I told them.

'Have you done your homework?' asked my dad.

'Yeah – and more too.'

'OK – don't be late,' ordered my mum.

'I won't and when I get back you'll still be on the sofa like two stuffed piglets watching *The Top Ten Reasons to Shave Your Eyebrows* or something.'

I ducked as a cushion flew past my head, smiled and left the house. Lisa was waiting for me at her door and we went straight up to her room.

'My dad's talking to his boss,' she told me.

'I'll be quiet as a mouse,' I replied.

When we got to her bedroom I jumped on her bed and lay back, pushing a T-shirt and bra to the floor.

'You should tidy up sometimes,' I said, but she ignored me, as usual. She sat down at her desk, on a swivel chair, and turned to face me.

'What's up then?' she asked.

'Nothing,' I lied. 'Can't I just come round to see you because I love you?'

'You *could* but you never do,' she pointed out. 'There's always a reason.'

I stuck out my bottom lip and pretended to sulk.

'Oh stop it!' she told me.

'Spoke to my mum and dad,' I said, smiling.

'Well done – you should get a Family of the Year award or something. Have your own reality show—'

'About Tyrone,' I continued, ignoring her sarcasm.

Her eyes widened. 'About Tyrone?' she repeated.

'That's what I said, sister.'

'But I thought you were too scared to—' she began.

'I didn't exactly talk to them about *Tyrone*,' I admitted. 'It was more of a . . . a general enquiry about stuff.'

'Uh-huh – exactly how *general*?' Lisa asked.

'General to the point of being . . . er . . . *sly*?'

She shook her head. 'So what exactly did you ask them and about who?'

I looked over, shrugged and told her.

DAVID

My cousin Satnam swerved his Audi around a car that was trying to pull out into the road. He swore at the driver, making comments about him being Muslim. Two other cousins were in the back – Inderjit and Jagtar, Uncle Malkit's lads. They laughed at him.

'Muzzy twat!' added Satnam, trying to prolong the laughs.

I shook my head and carried on watching the streets fly past. Satnam was giving me a lift home from a football team meeting, which, as usual, had been held in a pub on Melton Road. Not that anyone had been talking about football or the team. It was just an excuse to get pissed. My head was banging from the three pints I'd drunk and all I wanted to do was get home, away from my cousins and their stupid jokes.

'I gotta chat to you about summat,' Satnam said.

I shrugged. 'So chat . . .'

'Someone − and I ain't sayin' who − told me about that shit that happened at your school,' he told me.

'So?'

'So I heard it was a gang fight between some of our lot and a load of . . . er . . . blacks—'

'You mean *coons*?' shouted Inderjit from the back.

'*Blacks*,' repeated Satnam.

'What's that gotta do with me?' I asked, wondering where he was going with his chat.

'Your mate − that Dean—'

'What about him?' I snapped.

'Well, I've heard, from the horse's mouth, so to speak, that things are gonna get worse. Some good lads getting done for that − and their families ain't havin' it, you get me?'

I looked at him and shrugged. 'Me an' Dean wasn't involved − so it ain't none of our business, is it?'

'Could be,' said Satnam. 'If it gets into "them and us" . . .'

I shook my head. I should have known what he was going to say. 'It ain't about "them and us",' I told him. 'Or it is, but not the way that you think . . .'

Satnam looked at me. 'I don't get you,' he replied.

'It's *them* − all them man fighting an' that − and *us* − me and Dean . . . we's separate from that. And we ain't getting involved.'

Satnam shook his head. 'You're young, David − I know the boy is your mate an' that but when you get older − it's not the same . . . them *kaleh*, they ain't like us . . .'

'I'm not interested,' I told him.

'You will be when the shit goes down. When yer *kalah* mate is looking after his own. You'll be there like some likkle lap dog, watching an' that. Is that what you want? Where's your pride, man? You is *Desi* – homemade, bad bwoi stock . . .'

'He's my best mate from when we was yout's – you unnerstan'?'

'The bwoi even chats like him black,' shouted Inderjit from behind me.

'An' what accent was that you were putting on, you *knob*?' I said, turning to glare at him.

'Don't look at me like that – I'll give you a slap,' he threatened.

'Come on then!' I shouted back.

'*Enough!*' said Jagtar, who was my eldest cousin.

'Fuckin' knob,' I spat.

'Just calm down,' Satnam said. 'We're just trying to look out for you – that's all.'

'Well, you can do that by lettin' me out yer car – I'll walk the rest of the way.'

'Nah – we're only round the corner now,' replied Satnam.

'I don't give a f—'

'Just let him out,' said Jagtar. 'He'll soon realize himself.'

Satnam pulled in to the kerb and stopped.

'Don't count on it,' I told Jagtar. 'The one thing I ain't *ever* gonna be is like you . . .'

'You better stick to what you know, like everyone else,' he replied. 'You might get caught out otherwise and then it's us you gonna run to.'

He said a few more things too but I didn't catch them. Instead I gave the door an extra hard slam and walked off up the road, glad to be away from my family.

SIMRAN

My cousin Ruby pushed her way past a group of annoying Year Sevens and into our English class.

'Bloody kids!' she said, slamming her bag onto the desk and sitting down. Her long dark hair was tied in a bun and her school uniform looked like a sack over her skinny body. If you didn't know her you'd think she had an eating disorder but she didn't. She was naturally built like a twig. Between her and Lisa, I was freak girl.

Ruby hadn't been to school for a few days because she'd had flu and I asked her if she was feeling better.

'Kind of,' she replied. 'I feel a bit light headed and my throat is still really sore . . .'

'Shouldn't go round kissing frogs, should you?' I teased.

'Chance would be a fine thing,' she moaned.

'*Aaah!* Does Ruby want a boyfriend?'

She looked at me like I was mad. 'That was such a stupid voice,' she told me.

'Yeah – it was kind of silly, wasn't it?'

She nodded.

'There's something I want to talk to you about,' I said.

She began to pull books out of her bag as the rest of the class started to appear, including Lisa and Priti.

'What?' she asked absentmindedly.

I thought about telling her quickly but didn't get a chance. Lisa and Priti pulled up chairs and sat down.

'Hello!' they beamed at Ruby and me.

'Hey,' I replied.

'Everything OK?' asked Lisa. 'Only you weren't at the bus stop this morning.'

'Ruby's dad gave us a lift – sorry.'

'No prob – I didn't get the bus either. Dad dropped me off,' she said.

'So how did you know she wasn't at the bus stop?' asked Priti.

'Because I made my dad drive past to see if she was,' replied Lisa. 'I bet Ruby's dad didn't drive by to see if I wanted a lift – did he?'

I looked from Ruby to Lisa and then felt myself going red.

'It's all right, Simmy,' she said with a smile.

'Sorry, Lisa,' added Ruby.

'Families sticking together and all that,' replied Lisa.

For a moment I thought she was really pissed off but then she grinned and I knew that she was teasing us.

'*Cow!*'

'No need to get nasty, Simmy – I was only joking.'

'Moo . . .' I added.

Lisa stuck her tongue out at me as Mr Babbage walked in.

'What did you wanna tell me?' whispered Ruby.

'Later,' I whispered back, as Mr Babbage cleared his throat.

At lunch time I was sitting with Lisa when a fight broke out in the cafeteria. We were talking about Tyrone again, with me telling her that I wanted to speak to Ruby and Paula. Lisa was asking me why I felt the need to speak to the entire world about it when we heard a shout go up. I turned to see a lad called Pally, who was in my brother's year, dive onto another seated Asian lad. The table moved and then collapsed as they tried to punch each other. Suddenly a group of four male teachers ran over and began to separate them. But they were still kicking and punching, even when they had been pulled apart, and Pally was swearing in Punjabi – nasty, sexual things about the other lad's mum and sisters. He followed it up with a load of stuff about Muslims. The Muslim lad, who I recognized from our year, was going mad trying to get free, but two teachers held him tight and in the end he calmed down.

The other two teachers dragged Pally out of the cafeteria and down the main corridor, as the rest of the pupils sitting close by began to clear up the mess. I turned to Lisa and shook my head.

'Idiots,' I said.

'What was all that Punjabi stuff about?' she asked me.

'Usual stuff. Your mother's this and your sister's that . . . he's gonna get battered,' I replied.

'And what was that word he kept saying at the end? It sounded like *soolah* or something . . .'

'*Soollah* – it's a derogatory word, made up, I think, for Muslims,' I told her, slightly embarrassed and unsure of the reason why.

'So that was all about tribal shit again?' asked Lisa.

'Looks like it,' I said.

'Things are getting silly in this school,' she told me. 'Where's it gonna end – is it gonna be big-eared people versus small-eared next?'

'More like small willies versus small willies,' I replied.

Lisa giggled and turned back to her food.

'It's that Desi Posse again. I'm sure the Punjabi lad is one of them . . .' I said.

'The ones involved in that big fight? I thought they'd been kicked out.'

'Not all of them – haven't you seen the graffiti in the girls' toilets? Even the Punjabi girls are getting involved.'

'Yeah – but *why* are they getting involved? I heard some young lads the other day talking about the Desi Posse like they were heroes.'

I shrugged. 'I don't know why,' I told her. 'But there's definitely something going on.'

'Stupid . . .' said Lisa, forking a big pile of mash into her mouth.

She was right too. The Desi Posse *were* beginning to cause trouble with everyone and I just didn't understand it. A lot of the Punjabi girls at school were getting involved, talking about their own Desi Girls Crew, and drawing 'DP' onto their books and stuff. At first I'd just thought it was bit of harmless fun but it was getting past that now. I didn't know it at the time but the events of the next few months – the events in my own life – were going to send the Desi Posse and their nasty, violent prejudices over the edge.

I didn't manage to catch up with Ruby until after school. She was standing where she always did, waiting for her lift home. One of her brothers or her dad dropped her off and picked her up every day so she never got to hang out with the rest of us down the shops. She never walked home with us either and I knew she didn't like it.

'Hey!' I called out to her when I saw her by the railings.

'Do you want a lift back?' she asked me. 'My jailers should be here any minute.'

I shook my head. 'I'm going to walk back with the others,' I said. 'I wish you could too . . .'

'So do I,' said Ruby, looking sad.

'Let's tell them you're coming over to ours tomorrow,' I suggested. 'That way you can.'

Ruby thought about it. 'OK,' she said. 'I'll ask my dad—'

'Don't ask him,' I said. 'Just tell him – we *are* family, remember?'

Ruby shrugged and her shoulder bones looked like they might poke out of her jumper. 'Don't always help where I'm concerned,' she told me.

'Just do it and I'll tell Mum when I get in. That way she can call your mum and it's all sorted, isn't it?'

'Yeah,' she replied, although she didn't look too convinced. 'What did you want to talk to me about anyway?'

'Just stuff,' I told her. 'Got this boy after me and I was hoping to get your opinion on it, but we can chat about that tomorrow.'

I saw Parmjit, Ruby's eldest brother, pull up in some shiny flash car.

'Your ride's here,' I said, nodding in the direction of the car.

'Better go then,' she said, looking at me strangely.

'What's up?' I asked.

'This *guy* . . . ?'

'What about him?'

'Is he the black lad that some other girls told me about earlier?'

I looked at her in shock. I was about to ask her who had told her but she didn't let me.

'Because if it is – I don't wanna know. You're gonna get into serious trouble, Simmy.'

'But—' I began, only for Ruby to cut me off.

'It isn't right,' she said, as her brother leaned on the horn of his car impatiently. 'Call me later.' She turned to get into the car.

'You bet I will,' I snapped back.

I was fuming. Not only did I want to know who had told her, with my suspicions stopping at Priti; I also wanted to know why she was being all moralistic about it. I watched my cousin drive off and stomped back over to Lisa in a foul mood.

I was so pissed off that I called Ruby the moment I got in. She told me she was going up to her room and I heard her close the door behind her.

'It's just wrong,' she told me when she next spoke.

'What's wrong?'

'The whole thing – he's a *kalah*. Do you know what that means?'

'No – what *does* it mean?' I asked, getting angrier the longer I spoke to her but trying not to let it show too much.

'It means he's just after one thing – and it ain't worth the trouble.'

'One *thing*? So all black lads are the same, then?'

'Yeah, if I'm going to be honest,' Ruby said.

I couldn't contain myself. 'What the *hell* do you know about it? How many black lads you been out with?'

'That's not the point,' she said defensively.

'Yes it is – you're making judgements about a whole race of people based on *what*?'

'It's not racist,' she told me. 'It's about us being different . . .'

I tuned out for a while as she banged on, sick of hearing the same excuses for prejudice over and over again. When I tuned back in she was still off on one.

'. . . not worth the shit you'll get from the family. No one's gonna accept it – not even your old man—'

'What do you know?' I asked her. 'Just because your dad's like that don't make my dad the same.'

'Well, do what you like then,' she told me. 'But it won't work out right and you'll just get a reputation—'

'For what exactly?' I asked.

'For going out with *kaleh* – no *Desi* lad is gonna touch you afterwards.'

'That's just so fucking stupid,' I told her. 'What am I –

a piece of meat? That kind of thinking died with the Stone Age.'

'I'm just being honest – look, I've gotta go. I'll see you after school tomorrow anyway – we can talk about it then.'

I sat and thought for a moment and didn't reply. My mind was turning over and over what she'd been saying and I was confused about what to do. And then my mouth decided for me.

'Tomorrow's off,' I told her. 'I forgot – I'm going out . . .'

'*Oh!* What about another night?' she asked, not reading between the lines.

'I'll call you,' I said, snapping my phone shut on her.

I jumped off my bed and looked at myself in the mirror. Who was I going to be? Was I going to let other people decide my life for me or was I going to stand up for myself? I grinned at my reflection. Like I had any choice in the matter. I sat back down on my bed, picked up my phone and composed a text. When it was done, I sat and looked at it for a while. Then I shut my eyes, prayed for the best and sent it . . .

Later still I decided to tell Paula all about what was happening. Even though I didn't see her as often as I saw Lisa she was still one of my best friends and I wanted to find out what she thought, being black herself, about Tyrone and me. I was hoping for a positive response but what I got nearly knocked me off my feet.

'Describe this Tyrone to me,' she asked me over the phone.

'Huh?'

She giggled. 'Go on, Simmy – what does he look like?'

I waited a few moments, trying to get him right in my head, but Paula beat me to it. As I listened in amazement she described Tyrone perfectly.

'You *know* him?' I asked stupidly. It was obvious she did.

'Er, *yeah*!' she replied, and I could tell she was smiling on the other end of the phone.

'Am I missing something, Paula?'

'Only that he's my cousin, you silly moo,' she said, laughing.

'What?'

'My *cousin* – the son of my mother's sister – you know that weird concept – family an' all that.'

'No way!' I sat back on my bed, half of me smiling, the other nearly crying, although why I'll never know.

'Why would I lie about it?' Paula asked.

'I don't suppose you would,' I admitted.

'You wanna come over tomorrow to talk about it?' she offered.

'You better believe it,' I replied.

When the conversation was over I got up and paced my room. I couldn't believe what Paula had told me. I hadn't told David either, and he was best mates with Dean, who turned out to be the cousin of the boy I fancied. It was too much for me and I just had to call Lisa. Again. She answered on the second ring.

'Will you leave me alone, you witch!' she said.

LEICESTER MARKET,
NOVEMBER 1979

Gulbir Singh carefully sidestepped the gang of Mods hanging around at the entrance to the Malcolm Arcade, wary of the food he was carrying back to his market stall. One of the white boys, wearing a green parka coat and grey Sta-Press trousers with a sharp crease that looked like it could cut you, gave Gulbir a sneering look and asked him if he was related to Gunga Din. Gulbir ignored him and walked on, through the opposite arcade and back into the market, stopping at the kerb to let a blue Transit van pass by. The food and tea he was holding kept his hands warm in the biting cold wind.

Back at the stall he thanked Mr Abbas for looking after things.

'No problem,' replied Mr Abbas in Punjabi.

'How is the family?' asked Gulbir.

'*Inshallah* – they are well,' said Mr Abbas, as his son Ali appeared at his side.

'There's a man who wants to buy some things,' the boy told his father in English.

'*Saleyah!* Speak the language of your ancestors,' his father replied.

'No, no, *bhai-ji*,' said Gulbir Singh. 'Let the boy speak English – he will need it to get on in this country.'

'Maybe you are right,' agreed Mr Abbas.

Gulbir walked around the rails and into his stall, where his own son was sitting reading *Look-In* magazine.

'You brought food?' asked Mandip. 'But Mum made us food . . .'

'Sssh!' replied Gulbir, putting his left index finger to his lips. 'We can eat the other things later . . .'

'Did you get sausages and beans?' Mandip asked excitedly, happy to be sharing a secret with his dad.

Gulbir nodded and set the trays down on the stall bench, moving a pile of star-shaped price cards to one side.

'Just as you like it,' he told his son, who beamed at him.

'Where have Malkit and Rajbir gone today?' asked Mandip.

'Your brothers are at a market in Great Yarmouth,' replied his dad.

'When I'm as old as them will I have my own stall?' asked Mandip.

'If God wills it,' said Gulbir before taking a mouthful of sausage and egg.

By two in the afternoon, as the weather turned even colder, Gulbir realized that the number of gangs walking past the stall was growing. The football game started at three and the time for being extra cautious had arrived. Across from the stall, down past the huge pub that sat in the middle of the market square, a group of twenty or so skinheads had gathered. Gulbir watched as they stood around, drinking from cans of lager and swearing at passers-by, regardless of their colour. He saw the familiar face of Bhajno Kaur, the wife of his good friend Tarsem Singh, walking her two children past the gang. Sensing that they would need his help he shouted across to Mr Abbas.

'*Bhai* – get your cricket bat ready . . .' he told him.

'Why?'

Gulbir nodded at the gang and, just past them, the Asian woman and her children. 'Just in case,' he added to Mr Abbas, who nodded his understanding.

Mrs Kaur walked upright, shielding her children from the gang by walking between them. Suddenly an arc of lager sailed in her direction and she flinched. Her daughter saw what had happened and started to cry but Mrs Kaur took her hand and pulled her on, her son following behind. Gulbir felt his stomach tighten and the blood begin to boil in his head. He went into his stall, grabbed the old hockey stick that he kept for protection and walked back into the market. From where he was standing he heard Mrs Kaur swearing at the skinheads, who laughed at her and called her dirty things.

'Come!' shouted Mr Abbas. 'Let us get her—'

'One minute,' replied Gulbir, holding up his hand to stop his friend from charging forward.

They watched as the owner of a fruit and veg stall, a

white man, approached Mrs Kaur. He led her towards his stall, where his wife used a tea towel to clean her up. The man turned to the gang, walking up to one of the skinheads. He leaned forward and spoke to him and for a moment the skinhead squared his shoulders and clenched his fists, raring up to fight. But when the stallholder pointed back towards the stalls and the skinhead saw eight or nine other stallholders ready to defend their friend, his hands relaxed and his shoulders fell. He said something to his gang and they sloped away, heads down, like the children they were. Gulbir told Mr Abbas that he was going to make sure Mrs Kaur was OK.

'She's Tarsem's wife, is she not?' asked Mr Abbas.

'Yes, she is,' replied Gulbir before turning to his son. 'Keep an eye on the stall and if you see any more NF, tell Uncle Abbas . . .'

'Yes, Daddy-ji,' replied Mandip.

He watched his father walk off to check on the woman and her children. From the opposite corner, at the entrance to the indoor area, he heard the deep rumble of a bass line and the beginnings of a reggae song, played by the black man who owned the record stall. He looked over and saw three tall black men standing round the stall, wearing round woolly hats that covered their thick, long, serpent-like twists of hair. Mandip knew that they were Rastas – Mikey had told him – but he still felt a pang of fear. He didn't know why – they just looked so different to everyone else. But then one of them turned and saw him staring and the man flashed a big smile and called out to him.

'Hail, mi likkle idren!'

Mandip glanced away quickly before looking back. The Rastaman smiled again and lit a big long cigarette. Behind him Mandip heard someone approach. He turned to see Ali.

'Your dad gone over there?' asked Mr Abbas's son.

'Yes.'

'Good,' said Ali, walking into Mandip's dad's stall. Mandip followed.

Inside, with the rows of clothes hanging from the metal racks hiding them from the outside, Ali pulled a crumpled cigarette from his pocket. He straightened it out and then took a box of matches from another pocket.

'Where did you get that?' asked Mandip, as Ali, who was four years older than him, lit up.

Ali grinned. 'My dad – here, try it . . .'

Mandip shook his head.

'Go on! It ain't going to kill you, you chicken.'

Mandip hesitated for a moment before he took the burning stick from his friend. He put it to his mouth and did what he had seen Ali do. The smoke was thick and strong and it made him choke. He spluttered and coughed, dropping the cigarette as his eyes started to water. Ali broke into laughter, rescuing the tab from the floor.

'You need to practise,' he told Mandip, taking a drag.

Through the coughing and the watery eyes, Mandip nodded as he heard a popular tune begin filtering out of the huge bass bins of the reggae stall.

SIMRAN

'Took yer time, sister,' Tyrone said, as we sat in a coffee shop in town.

'I was on time,' I said, smiling because I knew that wasn't what he'd meant. And because I knew something about him, thanks to Paula, that he didn't.

'About callin' me,' he said.

'I knew what you were saying – I was just playin' . . .'

'Man – you can rhyme an' all.' He grinned.

'That was quite good, wasn't it?'

He looked into my eyes and smiled, and I felt my knees go weak like I was in some lame Hollywood chick flick. I blushed. He was so beautiful. Big brown eyes that reflected the light and skin like the purest milk chocolate, with not a blemish on it. I started to get a bit paranoid about the two small pimples on my chin, so small that you'd need a microscope to detect them.

'It wasn't bad,' he said, catching me in my daydream.

'What?' I asked, staring into his eyes.

'The rhyme, sister. Might make a rapper out of you yet . . .'

'But I don't want to be a rapper,' I told him. 'I want to be a forensic scientist.'

He gave me a funny look. 'A forensic *scientist*?' he repeated.

'That's what I said, boy.'

Tyrone looked away and then back at me. 'I don't like bein' called boy.'

'OK then – I'll call you girl.'

'Whatever,' he said.

'What's wrong with "boy" anyway?' I asked him.

'I just hate it. I'm called that all the time at school, you get me. The other lads get called by their first names and I get called boy,' he explained.

'Surely not *all* the time?'

'Yep – ever since I was a kid. It winds me up . . .' he added.

'OK – from now on I won't call you boy – ever.'

He took a sip of his mochaccino before he spoke again, not realizing that he'd left himself with a froth moustache.

'So why a forensic scientist?'

I smiled and pulled a tissue out of my bag, leaning across the table. For a moment Tyrone looked a bit scared, but as I wiped his moustache away he grinned.

'*Easy, sister!* Not in public – we'll get a room,' he joked.

'You *wish*,' I said, sitting back and screwing up the tissue. I put it down by my coffee cup.

'So stop changing the subject.'

I looked at him and smiled. 'You never seen *CSI*?'

'That thing with all the dead people bein' cut up and shit? Yeah – I seen it . . .'

'Well, I want to be one of them,' I said.

'A cut-up dead person?'

'No, you shithead, a forensic scientist. The person doing the investigating,' I explained.

'*Eh!* That's nasty . . . Now why would someone as fine as you want to go getting involved in some weird shit like that?' he asked.

'It's not weird,' I protested. 'It's a science like any other, only a bit more interesting. Imagine finding out how someone was killed just by what his or her body is telling you? It's cool . . .'

Tyrone shook his head and laughed. 'Nah . . . it's weird. And I'm just gonna take these away from you before you get any ideas.'

He reached across and picked up the spoon on my saucer and the plastic fork that I'd used to eat the 'half-fat but still not good for you' muffin Tyrone had bought me.

'Oh, stop being such a baby about it. I'm not gonna practise on you, am I?' I told him.

'You can if you like – just pretend and that . . .' he said with a sly grin.

'Like doctors and nurses?' I asked.

'Huh?'

'That game you play when you're kids?'

He shook his head. 'Weren't playin' no doctors and nurses game when I was a yout'.'

'So what did you play?' I asked.

'Cops and robbers – good stuff like that . . .'

'You boys – I mean *lads* – you're all the same.'

'No we're not – some of us is far more sophisticated than others . . .'

'*Ooh* – check you out,' I teased.

He sighed. 'Come on – finish that coffee before it turns into fossil fuel.'

I raised an eyebrow. 'Why – we goin' somewhere?' I asked.

'Yep.'

'*Where?*'

He shook his head again. 'When we get there,' he said, before putting down his own drink.

Tyrone's surprise venue was a pool hall on the other side of town, just behind The Shires shopping centre. We walked there and a couple of times Tyrone tried to take hold of my hand. But each time I pushed his hand away. I wasn't ready to be seen walking through town, even when it was half empty, hand-in-hand with a boy who wasn't actually my boyfriend. If we ended up seeing each other then it was cool, but until then . . .

We walked through the doors of the pool hall and over to the round bar, set in the middle of the room. The lighting wasn't exactly subtle. Each table was covered in a blue, red or orange cloth and the lights around the sides of the room were bright white or neon. Each bit of space on the walls was covered with American memorabilia – you know the sort of thing: posters of movies, Jack Daniels, Coca-Cola and Budweiser beer signs. It was kind of tacky, if I'm honest, but I didn't mind at all. I'd played pool a few times with my dad and David, and secretly I quite liked it. I was quite good too. Not that I was going to tell Tyrone that.

After he'd paid for a session we took our cues, chalk and balls over to a bright orange table and set them down. Tyrone looked at me and grinned.

'So this is where you bring your first dates?' I asked. 'Nice . . .'

His face fell because he thought I was mocking him. 'Don't you like it here?' he asked. 'We can go and do something else if you want . . .'

I shook my head. 'I'm only teasing,' I admitted. 'I like pool.'

'So there's no problem then, sister,' he replied, smiling again.

'You come here much?' I asked.

'Yeah, loads – me and my mates hang out in here . . . one of them works here . . .'

'Oh, right,' I said, catching a glimpse of myself in a mirrored sign for something called Dr Nuts soda. My hair looked a mess from what I could see and I decided to go to the loo and sort myself out.

'Just poppin' to the ladies,' I told Tyrone.

'You want me to get you a drink?' he asked.

'Yeah,' I smiled. 'Why not?'

'Anythin' in particular?'

'Surprise me . . .' I told him.

I followed the signs back out into the main part of the complex, which was a bowling alley, and found the ladies. There were two girls at the mirror, both Asian, and as I squeezed alongside them, careful not to nudge anyone, they gave me funny looks. I ignored them and sorted my hair out, before pulling some perfume out of my handbag – Dolce e Gabbana; expensive stuff that I'd got for Christmas from a boy at school called Hardeep. I hadn't even been going out with him at the time but I didn't worry about it. His dad was one of the richest men in our city and, as Lisa pointed out more than once, he could afford it. I sprayed just a touch of the sweet-smelling perfume onto my neck and put it away again.

'Best be some fine boy,' said one of the girls to the other. Her tone was sneering.

I didn't reply because they looked like rough girls and I didn't want to get into any trouble with them.

'Yeah – that's some expensive shit, *innit*? I could do with some myself . . .'

The one that spoke first gave me an evil look. I looked back for a second, before turning on my heels and walking out. I could hear them laughing and slagging me off behind my back.

'Lucky we didn't mash her up, you get me?' I heard one of them say just before the toilet doors closed behind me.

I walked slowly back towards the pool hall, angry but not frightened. I hated girls like that. Back by the table, Tyrone was waiting. He nodded at a small table by some low stools and grinned.

'Drinks for the lady,' he said.

I looked down and saw two bottles of Bacardi Breezer. 'I didn't – you didn't have to spend all that money . . .

Coke would have been fine,' I said, even though I liked a drink now and then.

Tyrone shrugged. 'It's a date – gotta have a few drinks . . .' He lifted his own bottle of Holsten Pils to his mouth and took a swig.

'Don't be thinking about getting me drunk,' I told him. 'I'll still whip your ass at pool.'

He grinned some more. 'Can't wait . . .' he said.

I lay back on my bed and waited for Lisa to reply.

'He did what?' she asked.

'Kissed me on the cheek,' I repeated.

'The *cheek*?'

'Yeah – and then he said that he'd call me and walked off.'

'The cheek – not the lips?'

'It was only our first date,' I pointed out.

I knew that she was shaking her head on the other end of the line.

'No tongue action?'

'Lisa!'

'Oh come on! You could at least have had a grope. He's got that fine body on him too – like an athlete,' she continued.

'I can't believe you . . .' I said.

'Did he smell nice?' she asked.

'Yeah . . . all clean and fresh and he was wearing some really nice aftershave.'

'What did it smell like?'

I thought about it for a moment. 'Like cloves and spices and stuff. A bit woody . . .'

'And did he have one?' she added.

'What?'

'A woody.' She giggled.

'Huh?'

'*Doh!* An erection . . .'

'Right, that's it! I'm not talking to you if you're going to be all dirty, girl,' I told her, feeling myself blush.

'Oh, don't be like that – I was only being . . .'

'Dirty?' I repeated.

'Chatty,' she corrected. 'Us girls have got to talk – it's what we do.'

'Tomorrow,' I told her.

'OK then, but you better not leave anything out – especially with all the "cousin of your other friend and possible family friend" confusion,' she insisted.

'There *isn't* anything to leave out,' I protested for the tenth time since I'd called her. 'You know everything I do.'

'You say that now, but I know you,' Lisa replied. 'You're probably hiding stuff from me just like you're hiding it from your brother.'

'I'm not telling *him*! He never tells me anything, and anyway, he'll just take the piss. I'll wait until I'm sure there's something there with Tyrone and me . . .'

'Yeah – I bet . . . You should tell David, Simmy. It's mean not to.'

'You just fancy my brother, you saucy cow—'

'*Don't!*'

'You so *do*!' I told her. 'It's *soooo* obvious.'

'Oh, get stuffed, you minger,' she said, like a spoiled child.

'Oh, go and poke your own eyes out, you hag,' I responded, matching her childishness pound for pound.

'Charming . . .'

I didn't reply to that. Instead I said goodbye and turned off my phone, settling back in bed to dream about Tyrone and his beautiful smile.

SIMRAN

Four weeks later . . .

Tyrone gave me a big smile and told me that he'd see me later.

I shrugged. 'I'm going straight home tonight,' I told him.

'Nah! And there I was – ready to take you out . . .'

'Can't,' I replied. 'I've got too much homework to do.'

'Forget about it,' he said. 'It'll still be there tomorrow.'

'Yeah, and I'll be in big trouble because that's when it's due in.'

Tyrone shrugged. 'Oh, right,' he said. 'In that case you best do it.'

I looked at him with a raised eyebrow. 'Don't you ever get homework?'

'Yeah – all the time,' he replied.

'I never hear you talking about it,' I said.

It was true. I'd been seeing Tyrone for just over a month and he hadn't mentioned schoolwork once. And he always seemed to be out doing something. If he wasn't with me, he was with his mates or playing football.

'I just do it when I get it,' he said. 'I'm kind of irritating like that – I don't find any of it that hard.'

'None of it – not even maths?' I asked, amazed.

'Nah – especially not maths. It's easy,' he told me, without a hint of bravado.

'So can you help me with mine then?'

'Anytime you like, Simmy. Just invite me round . . .'

I looked away. Some younger kids from my school walked past; one or two of them were staring.

'I can't do that,' I said. 'I told you that I'm not sure whether my parents will be happy about me seeing someone . . .'

'Well then, you'll have to come over to mine one day,' he suggested.

'Would your parents be OK with that?' I asked.

'Yeah . . . don't see why not,' he replied.

'So you don't know . . .' I said.

'Why would they mind?' he asked me. 'Ain't like you're some ugly monster from outer space – my dad would probably chat you up.'

I smiled.

'So when we goin' out then?'

'Maybe at the weekend,' I said. 'We could go into town or watch a film or something . . .'

'What – I gotta wait three whole days?' He gave me his 'little boy lost' look.

'Don't pout,' I told him. 'You look stupid . . .'

He grinned. Then something in his face changed and he told me that he had to go.

'You said that a few minutes ago,' I reminded him.

He looked past me down the road, and when I turned to find out what he was looking at, I saw a couple of Punjabi lads from my school.

'Something wrong?' I asked Tyrone.

'Nah – I just don't wanna be late,' he said.

I looked back at the lads and knew that Tyrone was lying. But I didn't say anything. I didn't want them to see me with Tyrone anyway. They were part of the Desi Posse and I knew they would give me grief for being with Tyrone – especially as he had been one of the lads involved in the big fight outside our school. The problem was I hadn't spoken to Tyrone about the fight or the fact that I'd seen him there. For some reason I just hadn't brought the subject up – just like I hadn't talked about my family too much or told him about the warnings that Priti and Ruby had given me. The way I looked at it, all of that stuff was nonsense anyway. We'd deal with it if it became a problem, not make it one in the first place.

Tyrone shrugged and told me that he'd call me later. Then he walked off, not even kissing me goodbye. I didn't mind. The two Punjabi lads were getting closer and I didn't want to attract their attention. Not that I had a choice. The older one, Pally – the one who'd had the fight in the dinner hall – walked up to me and said hello.

'Hi,' I said, not stopping.

'You ever go to gigs?' he asked me, matching my stride step for step.

'What gigs?' I asked, looking at his stick legs and

ridiculously big trainers. He had to be having a laugh, dressed like that.

'You know – bhangra and that.'

He said 'bhangra' with a Punjabi accent and for some reason that wound me up. I don't even know why.

'Not really,' I said. 'I prefer urban . . .'

'They play all that too, sister,' he told me.

'Who does?'

Pally went into his bag and pulled out a flyer for a club night. 'Desi Connection, man. The baddest crew in the area.' He offered me the flyer but I shook my head.

'Like I told you – not my thing . . .'

Pally grinned. 'Take it anyway, sister – I'll take you if you like . . .'

I looked at him and then shook my head. 'Not interested,' I said.

'Not yet, maybe,' he replied. 'But I'll give you my number anyways.'

He pulled out a pen and wrote a number on the flyer. Then he thrust it into my hand. 'All free too,' he said. 'My cousin is the promoter – got Jazzy B comin' down and everything.'

'Who?'

'What do you mean *who*?' he asked, looking shocked.

'I don't know who that is,' I admitted.

'Now you definitely gotta come to the gig,' he told me.

I shook my head. 'Don't think so.'

'Well, you got my number if you change your mind,' he said. 'Fit girl like you should be out and about, you get me?'

I lied and said that I would think about it before walking away, feeling slightly uncomfortable. I knew they were watching me and it didn't feel good, so I walked faster.

'Don't forget to call me!' Pally shouted after me.

'In yer dreams, dickhead,' I muttered to myself.

Ruby was waiting for me when I got back into school for afternoon lessons. I hadn't told her I was going out with Tyrone so she still thought that I was thinking about it. And she was doing my head in, referring to it over and over again. I took my seat in English and waited for her to start. I was in a bad mood and I couldn't work out why. The kind of mood that might make me say something I would regret. Luckily for me, Lisa was there too and Ruby didn't mention Tyrone once. Instead she started telling me about the same gig that Pally had been on about.

'Sounds wicked,' she said to us, as Priti walked in and sat down next to her, looking like her twin. They were as skinny as each other.

'What does?' Priti asked, pushing back her long curly hair.

'Some bhangra gig,' Lisa told her.

'*Yeah* – when's that on?' asked Priti, getting excited.

'Week on Saturday . . .'

As she said it, a light went on in my head and I had a brainwave. One that I decided to keep to myself until I got Lisa on her own.

'Whose gig?' Priti asked.

'That Desi Connection crew,' Ruby told her. 'Jazzy B's playin' . . .'

'Wow!' replied Priti. 'You going?'

Ruby looked at me and went red. There was no way she was going. Not with her strict parents and her stupid brothers.

'Er . . . I'm not sure,' she lied. 'Might have a family party on the same night . . .'

'You've always got family parties on,' said Lisa.

'Yeah – so what?' snapped Ruby defensively.

'She was only saying,' I snapped back. 'There's no need to be catty about it.'

'I wasn't,' Ruby replied. 'It's just that I think family is important, that's all.'

'Well, I'm going,' said Priti. 'What about you two?' She looked from me to Lisa.

'Not me,' Lisa replied. 'Not my thing really.'

'Oh go on, it'll be fun,' said Priti.

'Not for me,' Lisa told her. 'I can't do the dance moves and I don't like the music – and I'll be one of about three white girls in the place.'

'You'll be fine,' said Priti.

'Yeah, I know I will,' replied Lisa. 'Because I won't be there.'

'Suit yourself,' answered Priti.

'I will,' whispered Lisa.

Mrs Davis, our English teacher, asked us to be quiet and started the lesson. I looked at Lisa and then out of the window, as the teacher began to drone on about the book we were looking at. I didn't pay any attention. Instead, I thought about Tyrone and asking him about the fight, and I wondered when to tell Ruby that I was seeing him. We'd always been close as kids but I could feel us drifting apart, especially as I couldn't tell her half the things that I could tell Lisa. And her attitude towards black lads was making me question whether I even liked her at all. But it was calm before the storm time. Things were going to get much worse . . .

DAVID

I watched Dean as he tried to get away from Leanne. I'd turned up at the community centre after he called me, telling me that he had some big news for me. Ten minutes later and he was still attached to the girl like some kind of limpet. Not that Leanne minded. She was all over Dean like a rash and I was tempted to tell them to go somewhere private. In the end Dean snogged her again and then walked over to me looking sheepish.

'I can't believe you're kissing up that girl in public – like some twelve-year-old,' I told him.

'Can't help it if the girl loses her cool when I'm around,' he said with a smile.

'You wanna go somewhere private, bro. That Leanne looked like she was trying to eat you.'

Dean grinned. 'I wish . . .' he said.

'So what – you checkin' her now?' I asked.

'Nah – she's just one of many in my little harem,' he bragged.

'You wanna watch that,' I told him. 'You'll get caught out and you know who used to look after harems, don't you?'

'Who?' he asked, looking puzzled.

'Eunuchs.'

'Huh?'

'Men with them balls chopped off – which is what's gonna happen to you if you get catch—'

'Move with that!' he shouted, pulling a disgusted face.

'Just tellin' you,' I joked.

'Well, keep that shit to yourself, bro. Ain't no need for my brain to even entertain them thoughts, you get me?'

'So what you got to tell me that's so urgent? I was doin' my coursework,' I said.

Dean grinned even more broadly than before. 'Come,' he said. 'I'll tell you on the way home.'

'What?'

'I need to get back, bro. Got enough coursework of my own to do and my dad's doin' his nut over it.'

I shook my head. 'So you just asked me to walk all this way when you was thinking of heading back?' I asked.

'Yeah . . .'

'But you could have just passed by mine on the way home.'

'I could . . .' he began, only to trail off, as though someone had cut a string in his brain – the one that was holding his last train of thought.

'You knob.'

'Yeah, and talking of knobs . . .' he said, before coming

out with a whole load of nasty thoughts about Leanne and what he was going to do with her.

His dad opened the door and gave us both a funny look. 'Haven't you got any homework to do?' he asked.

'Hello to you an' all, Mr Ricketts,' I said, being cheeky.

'Don't play the fool, David. Your dad told me about the skiving.'

I looked at Dean and shook my head. 'I can't believe it,' I said to him. 'Now I'm gonna have to bear the stigma of being the son of a grass – I can't believe it . . .'

'We should shave your hair off – see if you've got a big letter G as a birthmark – like the anti-Christ—'

'That was six-six-six,' corrected Mr Ricketts. 'And you'll have some serious marks on your backside if you don't get your work done.'

I looked at Dean and grinned. 'Gutted,' I teased.

'I meant both of you,' said Mr Ricketts.

'Oh . . .' I said, not sure whether he was joking or not.

We walked into the living room and Dean's dad sat down. The television was on, showing that millionaire programme, but the sound was turned way down low so that Mr Ricketts could hear the George Clinton CD he was playing. I knew who it was because my old man liked him too – some weirdo old bloke in strange clothes singing about spacemen and freaky girls.

'What you doin' home anyway?' asked Dean. 'I didn't think your shift was done until late.'

'Got sent home early,' he said. 'Something about lack of work . . .'

'So my old man is home too?' I asked.

'Yeah, I gave him a lift. That heap of rust he calls a car broke down outside work.'

'Great,' I said. 'Not only is he on short hours but the car's knackered an' all – he's gonna be in a shit mood.'

Mr Ricketts glared at me. 'That language is not allowed in this house, David.'

'Er . . . sorry, Mr Ricketts.'

'Check out Mr Hypocrite.' Dean laughed. 'Like you never swear, Dad. What about when them BNP shitheads came to the door during the election? You was goin' mad, effin' and blindin'.'

'That's different,' replied his dad. 'And I thought I told you to go and do some work . . .'

'Just goin' . . .' said Dean, ushering me out of the room.

Up in his bedroom he told me his news and it was a shock. The Sunday league team that he played for, Hillfields, had been drawn against mine in a local league cup competition.

'But you lot got knocked out in the last round,' I pointed out. 'So how can you be playing against us on Sunday?'

'The team that beat us . . .'

'The Red Lion.'

'Yeah – them pussy bwoi – they got suspended for fielding three players who were banned—'

'*What?*'

'Yeah . . . three of their team were on bans but they played under different names – someone grassed them up to the league,' he told me.

'Who done that?' I asked.

'Our coach, Clarky – one of the banned players was sent off for punching him.'

'He punched your coach?'

'Yeah, and Clarky recognized him.'

'That's bang out of order,' I said.

'Yep – so you playin' on Sunday?' asked Dean.

'I think so . . .'

'So am I – should be a laugh.'

I thought about my stupid cousins and their racist attitudes and in my head I disagreed with Dean but I didn't say anything. Sunday had the potential to turn into a nightmare and I was tempted to ring my cousin Satnam and tell him that I was pulling out.

'You shot it or something?' Dean asked me.

'What?'

'You're just staring into space like a nutter,' he pointed out.

'Oh, right – nah, I was just thinking . . .'

'About how we're gonna beat you on Sunday?' laughed Dean.

'Yeah – dream on,' I said.

When I got home I rang Satnam to see if I was in the team.

'Sub at least, little brother – why?'

'I heard the Red Lion got kicked out,' I told him.

'Yep – we're playin' that Hillfields team.'

'The one my mate plays for,' I said.

'You on about that Dean?'

'Yeah,' I said. 'So you lot better watch your mouths . . .'

Satnam laughed. 'Don't worry about it. We'll be too

busy beatin' them to be callin' them names,' he told me.

'You'd better,' I warned. 'I ain't havin' no one dissing my best mate – I don't care who they are.'

'Relax, cos. What could go wrong?'

Everything, I thought to myself after I'd put down the phone. I couldn't see how my cousins and the rest of the team were gonna behave themselves when faced with an almost entirely black team. They were idiots. I should have been excited about playing in the cup against my best mate and his team but I wasn't. In fact I wasn't looking forward to the weekend at all.

SIMRAN

Tyrone looked at me and shrugged. 'We could go get something to eat,' he suggested. 'I'm starving.'

'Where?' I asked.

'There's this really good place on Market Street – does the best fry-ups in town.'

'Fry-ups – you mean sausages and bacon and stuff like that?' I turned up my nose.

'Yeah – they got salads and stuff too but a growing boy like me needs his calories,' he told me.

'You'll end up fat with blocked arteries,' I warned him jokingly.

'Never – I play football three times a week. Burn that shit right off.'

'Why eat it in the first place?' I asked.

'Better than a burger,' he said, grinning.

I watched a group of young girls walk past us as we stood by the clock tower in the city centre. They were dressed like clubbers, in short skirts, crop tops and full make-up. I wanted to ask them where the party was but I understood why they were dressed that way. Saturday afternoon in town was full of girls dressed to the nines, trying to catch the attention of the lads wandering around in groups. It was like a mating ritual or something. I smiled to myself.

'You smilin' at anything in particular?' asked Tyrone.

'No . . .' I replied. 'Just thinking about something . . .'

'What?'

'Oh, nothing important . . .'

'Well, if it's not that important can we go and get some food?' he asked.

'Yeah – but I'm not hungry. I'll just have a coffee or something.'

'Come on then,' he said impatiently.

We walked down the High Street, past a load of shops and then cut into an area called The Lanes, and on through a shopping arcade with a shoe shop at one end and a retro clothes store at the other. The retro store had a window display and I stopped to look at a bag that caught my eye.

'Can't we come back and look at that?' moaned Tyrone.

'Why don't you go on ahead?' I suggested. 'I know the place you mean so I'll catch you up. Just order me a drink.'

Tyrone looked unsure for a moment but then he nodded. 'OK – but don't be too long,' he said.

'Oh my *God* – possessive already,' I joked.

'*Nah!*' he protested, before realizing that I was having a laugh at his expense.

'See you in a bit,' I said, walking into the shop.

The girl working behind the counter didn't look like she was old enough to be there and she obviously bought all her clothes from where she worked. She wore orange flared jeans and a short shirt that was pink with bright red flowers printed on it. Her hair was tied up on her head and she had loads of piercings. She looked good with it all too – like it was her own, personal style, which she wore well. I smiled at her and asked how much the bag was.

'Thirty pounds – it's a nineteen seventies original,' she told me.

'Don't think I can afford that,' I admitted. 'What's the logo on the front?'

She told me that it was a silhouette of the three actresses from *Charlie's Angels* – the original TV show, not the Hollywood remake. I picked it up to get a closer look, realizing that it was a bit battered around the edges.

'I think I'll leave it,' I said. 'But I might have a look around.'

'Help yourself,' said the girl with a smile. 'Just shout if you need anything . . .'

She spoke with a slight lisp, which I realized was due to a stud that she had in her tongue. I wondered whether it hurt but didn't ask her. She probably got asked the same question about ten times a day. Instead I walked over to the clothes and looked through them, trying to find some-thing that went with the clothes I already had. In the end I found a fitted white shirt with a gorgeous flower design on it. It was only ten pounds so I decided to buy it, visualizing in my head the way it would go with three outfits that I had.

'That's lovely,' said the girl. 'I was thinking of buying it myself.'

'Oh,' I said, feeling guilty for some stupid reason. 'I don't *have* to take it . . .'

The girl shook her head and smiled. 'Don't be silly – and besides, it suits your colouring better than mine. It'll make your lovely skin tone stand out.'

I blushed, not knowing how to reply.

'I could never be your colour – I go all red and blotchy in the sun.'

'I was born this way,' I said.

'Lucky *you*,' replied the girl. 'Tell you what – give me a fiver for it.'

'*Really?*' I said, surprised.

'Yeah . . .'

'But won't you get into trouble with your boss?' I asked, worried.

The girl laughed. 'No – it's my mum's shop.'

'Oh – *thank you*!' I gushed.

'No problem. And come back again,' she said, handing me a five-pound note I hadn't been expecting.

'Yeah – I will,' I said. 'My best mate would love it in here.'

'See ya . . .'

'Yeah, bye,' I said, before walking out of the shop with a spring in my step.

There was something really great about complete strangers who were kind for no reason. It made me feel happy about the world. I smiled to myself as I walked through St Martin's Square, on my way to meet my lovely boyfriend. The smile lasted until just after I'd left the square and passed a small sweetshop. Then it disappeared.

Up ahead of me, standing by a pub, was Tyrone, talking to some friends. Only that wasn't the reason why I'd lost my smile. Walking past him and towards me were my uncle Rajbir and his wife, Jagwant, Ruby's parents. I looked at Tyrone, who hadn't seen me, and then back at my relatives. I knew that I was going to have to talk to them but I was praying that Tyrone wouldn't see me and come over. And I *never* pray. My uncle half smiled when he got close to me and stopped.

'Hello, Simran,' he said in Punjabi. He was wearing a red baseball cap with matching shell suit. He looked stupid, especially as he was so short and round.

'Hi, Uncle-ji.'

My aunt said hello too, only in English, and then she asked me what I was doing.

'Just shopping,' I said. 'And going to meet a friend.'

'*Which* friend?' asked my aunt, acting all suspicious.

'Er . . . Lisa,' I lied, hoping that the skinny, ugly witch would disappear in a puff of smoke. And to cap it all, my aunt was wearing a shell suit too; only hers was purple. I *had* to get me a new family.

'The *goreeh* from school?' she said, just like I knew she would.

'Yeah – she's waiting for me . . .'

'You should be careful wandering around town on your own,' said my uncle, still in Punjabi.

'It's not a problem,' I said, looking past him at Tyrone, who was still talking to his mates.

'Maybe not for you but people will talk,' continued my uncle. 'And there are too many stupid boys around . . .'

He turned and looked over at Tyrone and his friends and then back at me.

'Bad people always hanging around,' he added.

'I'll be *fine*, Uncle-ji,' I said, being really polite but answering him in English, a language that he spoke well enough.

Suddenly I saw Tyrone looking right in my direction. I gulped down air as my stomach flipped somersaults.

'I'd better go,' I said in a hurry.

'Ruby tells me that she wants to stay at your house,' said my aunt.

I looked at her and wondered what she was on about. Then it dawned on me. Ruby wanted to go to the bhangra gig and had used me as cover – *without* asking me first. Not that it mattered. I automatically went into sly-mode, covering for my cousin as always.

'Er . . . yeah. I'm having a girls' night,' I said, praying that Ruby hadn't said something else, but my prayer was in vain.

'Oh – she told me that it was Priti's birthday and that you were going to Pizza Hut.'

Out of the corner of my eye I saw Tyrone begin to walk towards me. My heart started to race.

'Er . . . *yeah* – we're gonna do that and then we're going back to my house to have a sleepover,' I lied.

'Well, maybe I will call your mother,' said my aunt.

She never used my mother's name. It was always 'your mother' to us kids and 'your wife' to my dad. It was a sign of disrespect, one that wasn't obvious but was still there. The stupid cow.

'Yeah,' I said, giving her a false smile. 'Call her. She knows *all* about it . . .'

I knew that my mum would read between the lines when my aunt called and not let me down. She was cool like that. And anyway I had more pressing concerns. Tyrone was approaching fast, a big goofy grin on his face. I couldn't risk him talking to me in front of Ruby's parents. I had to think fast.

'I've gotta run,' I blurted out.

'*But*—' began my aunt.

'Lisa's on her own, waiting for me,' I interrupted. 'And you know what town is like — all those *bad* people . . .'

I wanted to smile at the way I had used their stupid prejudices against them but I didn't have time. Tyrone was getting closer.

'Gotta go – bye!' I shouted as I turned round and ducked down Cank Street.

'Yes . . . goodbye,' my aunt said after me.

I still wasn't in the clear. If Tyrone shouted after me I was dead. I half walked, half ran down the street and into a delicatessen and coffee shop. Once I was inside I looked out into the street, praying that my uncle and aunt hadn't followed my route. They hadn't. Instead I got a very strange look from Tyrone as he entered the deli.

'What's up with *you*?' he asked.

'Huh?' I replied, playing dumb.

'You saw me and ran off.'

'Saw you *where*?' I asked.

'When you were talking to that Asian couple . . .' He gave me another funny look.

'Didn't see you,' I said, lying and feeling instantly guilty about it.

'You must be blind then,' he replied.

'Like a bat – didn't you know?' I said, smiling and hoping that he'd leave it at that. He did.

'Bats ain't blind,' he said.

'What?'

'Bats – technically they aren't blind. They don't see that *well* but they ain't blind – and they have this radar that—'

'I thought you were hungry,' I said, interrupting him.

'I am . . . but I ain't eating in here – it's all sandwiches and salad . . .'

'Well then, let's go to that other place . . .'

He gave me yet another strange look. 'Man – you always this funny?' he asked.

'Mad as a hatter,' I said, grinning and then giving him a kiss.

As we left, the assistant gave us a dirty look but I didn't mind. I checked for signs of my aunt and uncle but they'd gone. I gave Tyrone another kiss and my heart finally stopped trying to jump out of my mouth. I'd had a close shave and it didn't feel good. Tyrone just looked at me like I had two heads.

'Nutter,' he said, and grinned at me.

SIMRAN

'**Y**ou'll choke if you carry on eating like that.'
Tyrone shoved another forkful of bacon, sausage and egg into his mouth, ignoring me.

'And it's not very attractive,' I added.

'*Mmmffmmnn*,' he mumbled, spitting out a bit of egg.

'*Ew!*'

He chewed the rest of his mouthful before he spoke again. 'I'm hungry,' he told me, as if that made his messy eating OK.

'You're telling *me* . . .'

'Just drink your coffee,' he told me, preparing another mound of food.

'I like it cold – it tastes better.'

He swallowed again. 'I've got a football match tomorrow,' he told me.

'*And* . . . ?' I asked, pretending that I wasn't interested.

'Well, you did ask me what I was doing,' he reminded me, not that I remembered asking.

'*When?*'

'Yesterday – on the phone. Summat about goin' to the cinema,' he said.

'Oh yeah . . . Well, we can go afterwards – if you want.'

He shrugged, something he did quite a lot. 'Depends on how knackered I get. It's a cup game and we didn't know we were playing until yesterday.'

'Did you just forget?' I asked, as a couple of old women came and sat at the table next to ours. One of them gave Tyrone a funny look before turning away when she saw that I'd clocked her.

'Nah – we was knocked out in the last round but the team that beat us got kicked out for cheating,' he told me.

'Don't matter – I've got a load of work to do anyway,' I said, pretending that I wasn't bothered even though I was.

'So have I,' he replied. 'Got that coursework to do.'

'So we'll do something another day – what you doing next Saturday night?'

He gave me a surprised look. '*What?* I gotta wait *that* long to see you?' he asked.

'Don't be silly – we can see each other in the week. You're always waiting for me outside school anyway.'

'No I'm not,' he protested.

'*Yeah – right*. Every time I walk down to the shops you're there. Like a stray puppy,' I teased.

'There I was thinking you liked me and you go an' call me a dog,' he said, grinning.

'Call it like it is . . .' I said.

He shook his head. 'I reckon you enjoy dissin' me – like you're some kind of *freak* girl . . .'

I raised an eyebrow, wondering what he was on about. '*Hey?*'

'Yeah . . . like you get a kick out of being nasty. I bet you got a dungeon at home – complete with chains and whips like one of them freaky people.'

This time *I* shook my head. 'And you say *I'm* weird?'

'I could just call you after the game,' he said, changing the subject completely.

'You *could.*'

'OK – we'll do that and if we've got time we can go out.'

'*See?* You just can't get enough of me,' I joked.

Tyrone looked straight into my eyes and I felt my pulse quicken. He half stood, leaned across the table and gave me a long kiss. When I eventually opened my eyes, the two old women were giving us disgusted looks. Then I saw a middle-aged Asian couple at the next table along. You know that phrase – if looks could kill? Well, I was dead. The guy's eyes were nearly popping out of his head. Tyrone noticed too and he shook his head.

'Summat wrong, mate?' he asked the man, who looked away and then back at me.

'I *asked* if you got a problem,' Tyrone said, getting angry.

I stood up and grabbed my bag. 'Just leave it, babes – let's go,' I told him, trying to calm him down.

'In a minute . . . I wanna know what he's staring at first,' replied Tyrone.

'Forget it – he's just an idiot,' I said, taking hold of Tyrone's arm. 'Come on.'

Tyrone gave the man one last glare and then he followed me out. Behind us I heard the man call me a '*khungeree*', which is Punjabi for 'whore', and for a moment I wanted to go back in and slap him. But then I realized that Tyrone would go mad and I didn't want him to. I wanted to enjoy my time with him, not have it descend into violence over some stupid, ignorant arsehole.

'What did he say?' asked Tyrone as we walked back towards the city centre.

'Nothing,' I lied. 'He was talking to his wife . . .'

'Better not have said nuttin' either.'

'Just forget about it,' I said.

We were going to have to talk about people's reactions to our relationship at some point, I realized that. But it was too new and too fresh to get into all that heavy stuff. I just wanted us to have some fun. The problem was that other people were going to stop that from happening and there was nothing either of us could do about it.

I got home just after seven in the evening and went straight into the kitchen, where my dad was making chicken curry. My little brother Jay was in there too, trying to murder aliens on his PlayStation.

'*Smelly bum's back!*' he shouted when he saw me.

'You cheeky little bas—' I began, only for my dad to cut in.

'Simran . . . !'

'Sorry, Dad,' I said without meaning it.

I looked at Jay and gave him an evil glare but he just

115

smiled at me, tried and failed miserably to wink and then killed another alien.

'Chicken curry . . .' said my dad, in a mock Indian accent.

'You *look* like a chicken in them shorts,' I told him. 'Where'd you get them – some skateboarder shop?'

He looked down at his three-quarter-length trousers and then at me. 'Your mum got me these,' he said, sounding hurt. 'Height of fashion, she said.'

'Height of shite, more like—'

'Sim . . . not in front of the kid,' replied my dad.

'What kid?' asked Jay aggressively.

'You,' I told him.

'I'm *not* a kid . . . I'm *old*,' he protested.

'Not as old as Skateboard Dad over there,' I said, winking at him.

He grinned and tried hard to wink back but his facial muscles let him down again, and he looked instead like he was trying not to poo his pants.

'So what you been doing today?' my dad asked me, as he stirred his pot.

'Not a lot . . . saved the planet, stopped the extinction of the Bengal tiger and flew to Paris for lunch – what about you?'

'*Housework*,' he told me, pointing a chilli at me. 'What *you* should have done this morning . . .'

'Oh, *Dad* – I had to go into town,' I said. 'Girl's gotta have a life.'

'Not when I have to clean the bloody toilet,' he said, throwing the chilli back onto the worktop with the rest of the mess he'd made.

'*Ew!* You clean *toilets!*' giggled Jay. 'Homer's a toilet cleaner . . .'

'And I thought you said you were old?' I said to my little brother. 'You sound about five.'

'*Don't!*'

'Do.'

'At least I'm not ugly,' replied Jay as yet another alien went to its grave.

'How can you play that *and* look at me at the same time?' I asked.

'Same way you can pretend to be a good daughter and never clean the house,' said my dad.

'Oh, I'll do some tomorrow, you silly old man!'

My dad shook his head. '*No* – you'll do some now – starting in here.'

'But Dad – the whole place smells of curry. My hair'll end up stinking,' I moaned.

'Like your bum,' giggled Jay.

'Shut up, you stupid little git.'

My dad gave me another look and then asked me if had seen anyone interesting in town. For a moment I thought he knew about Tyrone and my heart sank but then I realized that he had spoken to his brother or his sister-in-law.

'Did Ruby's parents ring then?'

'Yeah ... something about her staying here next Saturday because you're having a party – I told them they must have been smoking dope—'

'*Dad!*'

'Only kidding. I figured she was using you as an excuse to get out of the house for a change so I told them it was my idea.'

'You *didn't . . .*' I said, disbelieving.

'*I did.*' He smiled.

I walked over and gave him a hug and a kiss.

'What's that for?' he asked, although I could tell that he liked it.

'*For being the bestest daddy-waddy in the whole wide world,*' I said, in the stupidest baby voice I could manage.

'Wass a *dope*?' asked Jay without looking up from the screen.

'You are,' replied my dad.

I went and sat at the table and poked Jay in the belly as he played. He pretended not to like it but then started to giggle as he wriggled about in his chair. I looked up at my dad and smiled again.

'I'm gonna have to call Ruby though,' I told him. 'She should have asked me first.'

'You don't have to,' he replied. 'Your uncle and aunt are bringing her over in about ten minutes.'

'What?'

'Yeah – your uncle says he's got an offer for me that I can't refuse.'

'I *bet . . .*' I said, with serious sarcasm.

'May as well hear what he's got to say,' he replied.

'*Great,*' I mumbled.

I didn't really want to see Ruby face to face because I was still upset with her for the things she'd said about black people, but I didn't have a choice. And besides, I had my own idea about what I was going to get up to the following Saturday night and she wasn't invited. Well, she *was* – but only as cover for me.

SIMRAN

My mum came home about a minute before Ruby and her parents arrived. I told her they were coming as soon as she walked through the kitchen door and her face fell.

'Why didn't you phone me?' she asked my dad.

'Thought it would be a nice surprise,' he replied, taking the piss.

'But the house is a mess,' complained my mum, looking flustered. 'And you know what she's like – bloody woman has her nose in every cupboard.' My mum always referred to my aunt as 'she' or 'her'.

'Well, I *was* telling your daughter that she should have done her chores,' said my dad, like it was my entire fault.

'How come she's always *my* daughter when she doesn't behave?' asked my mum.

My dad shrugged and smiled. 'Don't worry about it – I mean how *bad* can it possibly be?'

'You know what they're like,' my mum snapped. 'I haven't even got anything to give them with their tea . . . apart from biscuits.'

'So?' I asked.

'They'll complain like they did last time. Went and told your other aunt that I couldn't be bothered to feed them properly when they came over.'

'But who cares?' I said.

'Yeah – what are we supposed to do – run out and get them *samosas* just because they say they're coming round?' added my dad.

'Well, they're *your* family so if they complain they can take a running—' began my mum, only for the doorbell to interrupt her.

'Oh bloody hell – they're here already!' she said, glaring at my dad, who was still wearing her apron and cooking his curry.

'*What?*' he asked.

'Get the *door!*' she snapped.

'*I'll* get it,' I told them.

'In the living room,' said my mum. 'This place looks like a bombsite . . .'

I shook my head at my useless parents and went to let Ruby and her parents in. Ruby smiled at me nervously and said hello as I opened the door; her mum gave me a filthy look.

'Back from town?' she asked, raising her badly plucked eyebrows.

'No – I'm a clone,' I replied.

'Hello, Simran,' said my uncle in Punjabi. He was still in his shell suit but had lost the cap. It wasn't an improvement.

'Hi!' I answered breezily in English. 'Come into the living room.'

I led them in and immediately wished I hadn't. The room was a tip. Somehow my little brother had managed to leave half a sandwich, a bottle of Coke and a pair of what looked like his underpants on the table. I grabbed the pants and hid them behind my back, trying not to laugh, as my aunt brushed the sofa with her hand before sitting down.

'Your mother must be *very* busy at work,' she said slyly as she looked around the room in disgust, without even trying to hide her expression.

'I dunno,' I said, wishing that she would go and die somewhere, preferably in great pain. The stupid bitch.

'Where is my brother?' asked Uncle Rajbir, in Punjabi again.

'In the kitchen – making our food,' I told him, knowing that the thought of my dad cooking would wind him up. My uncle thought it was women's work. And it was one more reason for him to think that my mum was a witch – the git.

'So did you have fun in town?' asked Ruby, trying to lighten the mood as I prayed for one of my parents to come into the room and take over from me.

'Yeah – it was a *surprising* afternoon,' I told her, with emphasis.

'Oh,' replied Ruby, going a bit red.

'What is wrong with your face?' her mum asked.

'Nothing, Mum,' lied Ruby.

'We can pop up to my room in a bit,' I told her, not letting it go. 'Have a nice girlie *chat* . . .'

'Er . . . yeah, that would be good,' she said.

'Don't count on it,' I warned, watching Ruby's gaze drop to the floor.

Just then my parents walked in, together with Jay, who looked like he had been smartened up very quickly. Normally this involved him having his face washed and dried with a tea towel, and his hair slicked back with water. By the redness of his face I could tell that my mum hadn't given him any warning before she'd snatched him from his chair and shoved his head under the tap. He looked like he was still in shock. One minute he'd been murdering aliens by the dozen; the next he found himself standing in front of guests with wet hair, water trickling down his collar. Poor kid.

'Hello!' said my dad, in a madly happy voice.

I looked at my mum and grimaced.

I made the tea Indian-style, which involved standing at the cooker for ages watching milk and tea bags simmer and boil over and over again. At some point I threw in enough sugar to give a whale diabetes and then I strained it into a pot, trying not to scald myself. Ruby watched as I poured it and said nothing. When I was done I told her to grab a load of mugs and follow me back into the living room, where my mum had cleared the table. I wondered whether Ruby had seen me throw Jay's underpants behind the bin in the kitchen but then I realized she would have said something if she had. I would have. I didn't hear my mum talking to me.

'Simmy . . .?'

'Huh?' I asked dumbly.

'Biscuits?' said my mum slowly.

'Oh yeah . . . just getting them.'

I walked out of the room just as my aunt spoke, repeating what she'd said to me a little earlier.

'You must be *very* busy at work,' she said to my mum, looking round the room with her beady little eyes.

I stood just the other side of the door and listened in.

'What makes you say that?' asked my mum, brushing the seat she was sitting on with her hand.

'Well, obviously you have little time to tidy the house but what can you do – three children, full-time job?'

I waited to see how long it took my mum to reply. I knew that she was counting to ten to stop herself from throwing her mug at my aunt, and I followed her count. I got to eleven before my mum replied.

'Oh, you know how it is,' she said, through gritted teeth.

'No – I'm afraid I don't,' replied my aunt. 'I have no *need* to work. My husband provides all I need.' She emphasized her words with hand gestures and nodded her head from side to side. It was a really Indian thing to do.

'Well, I *enjoy* working,' said my mum. 'I'd get very bored if I just sat at home, getting more and more sour each day . . .'

'*Sour?*' asked my aunt. 'What is this meaning? I don't understand.'

'Oh, *nothing*. Too much time on your hands – nothing to do except *gossip* . . .' said my mum, beginning to lose it again.

'*Biscuit*, anyone?' asked my dad, saving the day. Then he shouted at me. 'Simran – hurry up!'

'On my way!' I shouted back, wondering what more the evening would bring.

I ended up in my room with Ruby and after about twenty minutes of faked normal chat we got round to discussing the gig the following Saturday, the one that Ruby had jumped the gun on.

'You should have asked me first,' I told her.

'I know – I'm sorry . . .' she said. 'Didn't think you'd mind.'

'It's OK,' I told her. 'Besides, we can do each other a favour.'

'I don't understand.'

I looked at her and smiled. 'I'm not coming to that bhangra gig – you know I'm not into it that much . . .'

Ruby's face fell. 'But then what's the point of—?' she began.

I cut her off. 'I'm going out to another place – a bar or something – with Lisa and that lad you disapprove of . . .' I said, waiting for her to reply.

'That *black* boy?'

'He's not a boy,' I told her. 'Priti and her mates are going to the gig anyway so you can catch up with them. And at the end of the night I'll come and meet you outside the gig and we can share a cab back here—'

'But I thought we were going together,' she said, looking confused.

'*No* – you and Priti said you were going; I didn't say a word.'

'Are you sure about seeing this black guy though?' she asked.

I wondered whether to admit that I was already seeing him but I decided against it. 'We're just going out for
a drink,' I lied. 'Nothing serious . . .'

'If you get caught—' said Ruby.

'By *who*?' I asked. 'And do I *care* anyway?'

'I can't believe you're . . . There's plenty of nice
Punjabi guys out there,' she told me.

'It's not about that. It's not like I go out looking only
for Punjabi guys or I went searching for some black lad. I
don't look at colour . . .'

'Well, I think you're making a mistake,' she said.

'Yeah, you've told me that already – and you know
what? I couldn't care less.'

'I don't mean to be nasty or anything. You're my
cousin – I'm just telling you how things work,' said Ruby.
'It's a taboo – I even saw a programme about it. *The Last
Taboo*—'

'You what?'

'It's the one thing that Asian parents ain't going to
accept. It's just wrong—'

'No – *you're* wrong,' I told her.

'We'll see,' she said. 'It's just my opinion – that's all.
They ain't like us—'

I heard her mum calling up to her, telling her that they
were leaving.

'Well, keep your opinions to yourself, Rube – otherwise we're gonna fall out and I don't want that.'

Ruby gave me a look and then shrugged. 'OK,' she
said.

After the visitors had gone I stayed in my room for a bit

and exchanged flirty text messages with Tyrone. Then I thought about Ruby and what she'd said about taboos. Wasn't that the point of them – to be broken? I went down about an hour later and I could hear the sound of dying aliens coming from the kitchen. I popped my head round the door and saw Jay. He was on his own.

'Where's Mum and Dad?' I asked him.

'In the living room, arguing,' he replied, not looking up.

'About what?'

He shrugged. 'I dunno – something Uncle Rajbir said . . .'

I left him where he was and went into the living room. My parents were sitting opposite one another, each of them looking at anything but the other, like big kids.

'What's up with you two?' I asked, plonking myself down on the sofa next to my mum and switching on the telly with the remote.

'Ask *him*,' said my mum childishly.

'Dad?' I said, knowing what he was going to say.

'Ask your mum,' he replied.

'Just tell me what's happened,' I told them.

My mum looked at my dad. 'They're *your* family – you tell her,' she said.

'I'm not the one who thinks that it's a big deal,' he replied.

'What's not a big deal?' I asked, beginning to feel worried. For a moment I thought my uncle and aunt had seen Tyrone and put two and two together.

'Your uncle offered me a job,' my dad finally told me.

'Oh right . . . so *what*? Ain't like he's never done that before.'

'Yes – only *this* time your father said yes,' my mum told me.

My uncles were always asking my dad to join the family business, which David and I jokingly called Gill Enterprises. They thought that my dad was strange with his crap factory job, as they put it, and his embarrassing old car. And then there was what they thought about my mum. My dad had always refused their offers in the past, which is why my mum was so shocked. So was I.

'*What?*' I asked, not believing my ears.

'He said he'd think about it,' continued my mum.

'Which *isn't* the same as saying yes, is it?' my dad pointed out.

'Might as well be,' she snapped.

I looked at my dad. 'I don't get it,' I said. 'I thought you weren't into what they do?'

'I might not have a choice,' he told me. 'I don't think the factory is going to be open much longer. We're already on short hours . . .'

'It'll be all right – it always is . . .' replied my mum.

My dad shook his head. 'Not this time,' he said. 'They reckon it's cheaper to make the parts we make abroad – we ask for too much money apparently, and the company we supply has gone into administration.'

'I didn't know that,' I admitted.

'I've been talking to Mikey about it and he's looking for another job too,' continued my dad.

'But working for your brothers . . . ?' said my mum. 'You'll go mad.'

127

'We can't survive on just your wages,' he told her. 'I've got to do *something*.'

My mum shrugged. 'You could retrain . . .'

'Or I could take up their offer,' he countered.

I looked at both of them in turn. 'Is anyone gonna tell me what their offer actually was?' I asked.

'They're taking on a sandwich shop franchise and they want me to have it. I just pay them back the start-up money over as long as it takes.'

'Huh?' I asked, being dumb.

'They're going to put the money in to start it,' explained my mum. 'And your dad is going to run it and pay back the money a little at a time—'

'Can you *do* that?' I asked.

'Your uncle thinks it'll work. He wants me to go round tomorrow and look at numbers and stuff . . .'

My mum shook her head again. 'After everything they've done and said, I can't *believe* you're even thinking about it,' she told him.

'They're still family and they wouldn't ask if they didn't care,' replied my dad. 'And like I said – we might not have any choice if I get made redundant . . .'

I wondered why my dad hadn't explained exactly how serious his work situation was. It had to be *really* bad for him to consider working with my uncles. My mum had a point though. They'd made my parents' life hell – said and done some really nasty things. And now they wanted to help us out? I didn't believe it. Not that it was going to happen anyway. My dad was never going to get the sandwich shop. And that would be my fault.

DAVID

I checked out my cousin Satnam's face as Dean walked over to us. He looked at me and then back at my best friend, as the wind whipped up and sprinted across the park, nearly taking me off my feet.

'Easy, bro!' shouted Dean through the gale.

'Yes, Dean,' I replied, smiling.

He stood in front of me, nodding towards Satnam.

'This is my cousin,' I told him. 'Satnam.'

'Easy,' said Dean.

'Awright . . .' replied Satnam, looking away.

I looked past Dean towards the rest of his team, who were warming up at the other end of the pitch. Hillfield Rangers was made up of mainly black lads with a couple of white brothers and an Asian lad whom I recognized.

'Is that Raggy?' I asked Dean.

'Yeah, man – he switched over to us this season,' he told me.

My cousin snorted. 'He's a traitor, man. Used to play for SEFC—' he said.

'*Who?*' I asked.

'Sahota Enterprises – you should know them. They's family . . .'

I shrugged. 'Man can play for anyone he wants,' I said. 'An' I ain't got no clue 'bout no Sahota team.'

Dean gave me a funny look, like he wanted to call my cousin a knob, but didn't, just to be polite. I knew exactly how he felt. Another blast of wind caught me as I spoke.

'He's good.'

'Wicked,' agreed Dean. 'Fast like a Ferrari and the ball sticks to his foot.'

'We got the man to tek care of him,' boasted Satnam. 'He ain't doin' shit this game.'

'Didn't he play youth for Leicester City?' I asked, recalling where I'd heard of him.

'Yeah – till last year . . .' said Dean.

'I heard he didn't have the balls for it,' said Satnam. 'Couldn't take the pace.'

'Nah – that ain't the story,' corrected Dean. 'He did his ligaments and they let him go.'

Satnam shrugged. 'Every man's got some excuse,' he said, grinning.

Dean didn't grin back. Instead he looked at me. 'Better go warm up,' he told me.

'If you can in this wind,' I said. 'The ball's gonna go everywhere.'

'As long as it goes in your goal,' he teased.

'We'll see, bro,' I told him. 'Good luck.'

'You too,' he said. 'We're goin' for a drink afterwards. You can come if you like . . .'

'Where?'

'The Horse,' he told me.

I nodded. 'We're all headin' in there anyway,' I said.

'In a bit,' he replied before turning and jogging back to his team mates.

Satnam gave me a funny look. 'He's a cocky fucker, ain't he?' he said.

'No more than you,' I replied, smiling to defuse the situation.

The rest of our team began to turn up and Satnam went over to them. I watched him go and began to stretch my hamstrings and calves, hoping that things would stay calm once the whistle blew and the game started. Not that there was much chance of that. I saw two more of my cousins, Parmjit and Inderjit, get out of an Audi A3, along with Suky Mann. The last person out of the car was Raji Mann, the self-styled head of the Desi Posse, with a fresh skinhead haircut. He was the one who'd been kicked out of school after the fight.

'Shit!' I said to myself, wondering what he was doing at the game. He drank too much booze and ate too many kebabs to play football.

Inderjit came towards me and smiled. 'Yes, little cos . . .'

'Ind – how you doin'?' I asked, wondering why his gold chain was on the outside of his tracksuit.

'Cool, man. You ready to give these *kaleh* a beatin'?'

'My best mate is playin' for them,' I told him, as a warning.

'So? This is football and we're here to win. You can be mates all you like after — you get me, blood?'

'Whatever — I'm just gonna play my game,' I said.

'Can't ask for no more,' Inderjit replied.

I nodded in Raji Mann's direction. 'What's *he* doin' here?'

My cousin turned and followed my line of sight. 'Who — kebab boy?' he asked.

'Yeah — Raji.'

'Come to watch the game, same as a lot of man. Why?'

'I don't like him — that's all,' I said.

Inderjit gave me his 'older cousin' look. He was about to lecture me on something.

'His father's sister is married to our dad's cousin — that makes him family,' he said, not joking.

'*Eh?*'

'He's family so there ain't nuttin' to dislike — *understand*?'

I laughed. 'His father's sister ... how many times removed is that?' I asked.

'That's some white boy shit you're chattin',' he told me. 'Indian man don't see it that way.'

'Good job I'm English then,' I replied, knowing that it would wind him up.

He shook his head, called me a few names in Punjabi and then walked back to his mates. The wind got even stronger, if it was possible. I turned away from the rest of them and wondered whether Dean's team needed players.

★ ★ ★

It took another twenty minutes for the referee to turn up and by that time both teams had a load of supporters cheering them on. The wind was charging across the park like a raging bull when we gathered together for a team briefing. Parmjit, who was looking after the team because the coach, Deggsy, was recovering from heart surgery, told us to huddle as he went over the tactics he'd planned.

'Four-four-two – just for the first half. They got fast wingers and we need to hold 'em in check. Come the second half they'll be tired and then we can change things . . .'

'Check out Mr Tactics,' joked the keeper, Amandeep.

'Time for jokes is later,' Satnam told him. 'Unless you come out to catch the ball at a corner, that is . . .'

The rest of us laughed and Amandeep went the strange shade of red that Punjabis go.

'We gotta stick to the game plan too. Not like last week . . .' continued Parmjit.

'Them white bastards were dirty,' said Amandeep, who had let in three soft goals in our previous league game.

'Nuttin' to do with bein' dirty,' Parmjit told him. 'We didn't keep the ball . . .'

'Yeah, let's try an' play like a team this week,' added Suky Mann, who was one of the substitutes. I had his place.

'Exactly,' agreed Parmjit. 'We gotta keep our shape. Last week you wankers was all over the place.'

Suky looked at me and sneered. 'An' if you get a chance, give them *kaleh* a good kicking,' he said, his eyes never leaving mine.

'Not when the ref is looking,' warned Parmjit.

'Fuckin' black, banana-eatin' monkey *bastards* . . .' spat another lad, Jas.

'There ain't no need for that,' I snapped, taking the bait.

'Yeah there is,' countered Suky Mann. 'Two of your black bum chums over there was responsible for my bro gettin' kicked out of school . . .'

A murmur went up as I stared Suky down. He held my gaze for about three seconds before he looked away – the pussy.

'You're the biggest dickhead I ever met,' I told him. 'I heard Raji got kicked out for being a fat, smelly, useless shit that couldn't even see his own prick 'cos his belly was so round.'

Suky looked at me again, his eyes blazing. 'That's my family you is on about,' he said. 'Carry on – see what a gwaan.'

'Seein' as how you hate black people so much, it's funny that you try an' talk black,' I told him, feeling my blood pressure begin to rise. I was about three seconds from walking off and letting them play without me.

Suky gave me another sneer and then looked at Satnam. 'I'm just sayin' – them niggers got to pay,' he said.

About half of the team said they agreed, while the rest looked on, embarrassed at the racist language maybe or just watching a beef brewing. I looked at Parmjit and my three seconds came bursting up, like a missile launched from a submarine. Red spots began to dance in front of my eyes.

'Fuck it!' I said, pushing the goalkeeper away from me. 'I ain't playin' for you wankers . . .'

'You gotta play!' shouted Parmjit, grabbing my arm, as I made to walk away.

'No I ain't! You can stick your team up your fat, hairy batty hole.'

He was about to say something else but stopped when he saw the ref coming over. 'Suky – get stripped,' he snapped.

I didn't turn round as I made my way to the sideline, threw off the team shirt, pulled on my hooded top, grabbed my bag and walked across to the Hillfields supporters. I had played my last game for my cousin's side.

DaVID

When Dean saw me standing with his team's supporters he gave me a funny look and a thumbs-up sign. I nodded to show him that everything was OK and watched my old team kick off. Someone tapped me on the shoulder and I turned to see an Asian lad that I knew.

'Easy, Ammo,' I said.

'What you doin' over here?' he asked.

'Ain't playin',' I said, shrugging.

'Been dropped?'

'Summat like that,' I replied.

'Well, you're with the winners now,' he bragged.

'Looks that way,' I said, turning back to the game.

Someone had kicked the ball up into the air and I saw Dean prepare to challenge for it when it came down. I also saw Suky eyeing Dean, not the ball, and when the challenge came, Dean ended up on his back, holding his face. The ref blew for a foul and ran over to Suky, who raised his hands like he hadn't done anything. I wanted to run on and head-butt him but I managed to stop myself. I knew what Dean was like and I waited patiently for him to get his revenge. It came five minutes later, just after my old team had missed an open goal, the striker, Dal, hitting the ball over the bar from about five yards out.

The Hillfields keeper hit a long kick and this time, as Suky went for the ball, Dean rose with him and caught Suky's cheek with his head. Suky screamed like a girl, hit the ground and rolled over about ten times. This time the ref gave Dean a yellow card and Suky had to leave the pitch before the game could restart. As soon as it did, the Hillfields right winger crossed the ball into the box and Raggy volleyed a powerful shot past Amandeep. The crowd went crazy, jumping up and down, as my old team mates blamed each other for the goal and Suky came back onto the pitch.

The first sending off came after the restart, when Jas, the left back for my cousin's team, punched the goal scorer in a scuffle. The referee spent about five minutes trying to calm it all down and a tall lad, who was playing midfield with Dean, pulled Raggy away. The referee gave a free kick, which Dean took, hitting the post with his effort. The half ended about fifteen minutes later.

The second half descended into madness from the first whistle. The tall lad playing with Dean got hold of the ball and skipped past four of our players, bearing down on goal. Suky slid in, both sets of studs showing, in a deliberate attempt to hurt him, but the lad saw it coming. He jinked to the left and put a low shot underneath

Amandeep's body for the second goal. My cousin Satnam went crazy, kicking out at the scorer as he ran past, celebrating his goal. Dean saw the kick and he squared up to my cousin, who started swearing at him. I didn't hear everything he said but I did make out the word 'monkey' and my stomach twisted and turned. I watched Dean's expression change to amazement and then to rage, and he decked my cousin with one punch. Suky Mann jumped in and everything went mad. The Hillfields supporters started booing and two of them, both older black men, ran on to try and calm things down. But Suky was punching at anything that moved and when Raji and some of the other Asian lads joined in, I thought it would end with the police being called.

It didn't though. After a long while, the ref regained control and sent off Satnam, Suky and Dean. When one of the other Hillfields players complained, he got a red card too. I looked at Ammo, who just shrugged.

'Weren't no need for that shit,' he told me.

'I know,' I replied, agreeing with him.

'That lad givin' it the mouth's yer cousin, ain't he?'

I felt myself going red as the embarrassment rose up inside me. 'Yeah . . . shame you can't pick yer family,' I said.

'Too right, bro,' he told me. 'I got 'nuff family like that.'

I waited for him to say something else but he didn't. Instead he shook his head and we watched the rest of the game, which ended with a third goal to Hillfields, scored by the tall lad in midfield again. He'd been the one on the receiving end of most of the dirty tackles so he enjoyed his second goal, running over to Dean and jumping on him to celebrate. Dean, who looked like he was still fuming, pumped the air with his fists. At the end some of my old team shook hands with the opposition but the rest just trudged off, swearing at the Hillfields players and each other. I watched them, pleased that I hadn't played for them. That I wouldn't be playing for them ever again.

After the game I walked over to the pub with Dean and the tall lad who'd scored twice. The rest of Dean's team were already there, along with a few fans, and I wondered if my old team would try and kick off because they viewed The Horse as their local and might think that Hillfields were gloating. They were stupid enough to see it that way. Dean asked me why I hadn't played as we crossed London Road to get to the pub, avoiding the fast-flowing traffic and a couple of boy racers in Peugeot 206s who were too busy trying to out-speed each other to notice that there were people crossing the road.

'Wankers!' I shouted after the speeding cars, hoping they'd run into a police trap further down the road.

'Never mind them,' said Dean. 'What happened to you?'

'I just decided not to play for them any more,' I told him.

I wanted to tell him the truth but I wasn't sure how. I knew that he wouldn't blame me for my team's attitude but I still didn't want to admit that I had been a part of their bullshit. Besides which I had a feeling that Suky, Raji, Satnam and the rest of them would show how bigoted they were at the pub anyway. After all, they'd already done it on the pitch.

'Was it because they're a bunch of racist bastards?' asked Dean, reading my mind.

'Yeah . . . I mean, I don't even think they really know what they're on about – you get me? It's just that they're so stupid they pick the most obvious things to say to people . . .'

'They called me a monkey all the way through the game,' said the tall lad.

'*See?* I can't play with them, man,' I replied.

Dean looked at his teammate and something passed between them. Then he stopped in his tracks. 'You see how rude I am, bro?' he said.

'What you on about?' I asked, as we all came to a stop about twenty metres from the pub entrance.

'I ain't even introduced you two yet.'

I looked at the tall lad and shrugged. 'Any friend of yours an' all that,' I told Dean, but he shook his head.

'Nah, man – this is my blood, blood – you get me?' he said.

I did but I wasn't sure anyone else would have.

'This lanky bwoi is my cousin – Tyrone,' he told me.

'Easy,' I said, smiling.

'An' this here,' he added, turning to Tyrone, 'is my other family . . . David.'

Tyrone stuck out a balled fist and I did the same, touching his with mine.

'I heard enough shit about you, man,' said Tyrone. 'You two are like joined at the hip or summat . . .'

'Since we was babies,' said Dean proudly. 'We's like fish an' chips, unnerstan'?'

I looked at Tyrone and we both burst out laughing.

'As long as you is the fish, bruv,' I said through my laughter. 'I ain't into smellin' like no haddock, you get me?'

'Ah – rest yuhself . . . you know what I mean . . .' replied Dean.

'Like salt an' pepper, cos?' asked Tyrone, taking the piss.

'Or left and right foot?' I added.

'Both of you can go suck my—' began Dean, only to stop mid-sentence as a couple of fit girls walked by.

'Yes, ladies . . .' He grinned.

The girls looked at him and giggled, walking away. One of them turned round and gave me a look, a big smile on her face. I smiled back. I recognized her from somewhere but couldn't recall where it was.

'Nah!' laughed Tyrone, mocking Dean. 'They diss you and give David here some kinda look.'

'Nah, nah, nah. They was checkin' *me* out,' insisted Dean, even though he knew he was wrong.

'In yer dreams, cos,' said Tyrone.

We walked into the pub and found the rest of the Hillfields team. To do this we had to walk past my cousins and I kept my head down as we passed by, ignoring them. But Satnam grabbed my arm.

'What you doin'?' he asked me.

'Havin' a drink with my mates,' I told him.

'We're your mates,' he told me. 'How many times we gotta tell you that?'

'I ain't interested,' I replied.

'Look, man. I'm sorry about all that shit from earlier but it don't mean nothing. It's just banter – you know how it goes . . .'

'Yeah,' I said, 'I know how it goes but it don't go that way for me, you get me?'

Satnam put his arm around me. 'Come on – you an' me are family. Ain't nothing can change that,' he insisted.

'Whatever – don't mean we have to be friends,' I said.

'But you're still part of the team,' he told me, not listening.

'Not no more I ain't. You can stick yer team.'

He let go of me, turned, put his pint down on the bar and then turned back to me. 'I ain't fuckin' wit' you now!' he snapped. 'I'm older than you and you best listen when I say—'

'Go fuck yourself,' I replied, walking over to join Dean.

Satnam said a few things in Punjabi – things I ignored because I didn't want to fight my own cousin, no matter how much I disliked him.

'What was all that about?' asked Dean as I rejoined him and his mates.

'Nothing,' I lied, taking the Coke he'd got for me.

Dean introduced me to one of his coaches, Simon. I said that I was looking for a new team and he told me to come to a training session the following week. The team was looking for new players and he said that Dean had mentioned me before. Simon bought us another drink and told me that he would see me in the week.

We walked over with Tyrone to play on a fruit machine in the entrance to a conservatory attached to the side of the main pub; we had to move every now and then as people walked in and out. We'd been playing for about ten minutes when Raji and Suky Mann kicked off. The first I saw of it was when Raji shoved past Tyrone, calling him a monkey in Punjabi. I span round to face him and told him to get lost.

'Fuck off, you traitor,' he spat at me.

Dean played another round on the machine and then joined in. 'Why don't you just back off wit' yer fat belly?' he told Raji.

Suky stepped between the two of them and shoved Dean back into the fruit machine. In my head things went into slow motion as Tyrone smacked Suky in the mouth. Raji jumped on Tyrone and they hit the ground, catching a table as they fell. The students at the table screamed as glasses and ashtrays smashed. I turned and saw Suky punch Dean straight on the nose and I felt my arms take on a life of their own.

I grabbed Suky and shoved him away and out of the side entrance to the conservatory, into the car park. He tried to get his hands free from the hold I had on him but I leaned back and head-butted him, breaking his nose. The cracking sound nearly made me puke and I had to let him go. He fell to the floor and put his hands to the bloody mess of his face.

That was when I felt the punch. It caught me on the back of the head and sent me crashing into Suky. I pushed him out of the way and sprang to my feet to see who had hit me. It was Satnam, my cousin. I swore at him and charged, shoving him into the door. He pushed me back but I managed to send an uppercut into his chin.

Then all hell broke loose. Both teams flooded into the car park, hitting each other with fists, feet and bottles. The landlord and two of the bar staff ran out too, trying to stop the fight, but they didn't have the strength.

In the end the landlord took out his mobile and called the police and everyone did a runner. In the midst of the fighting I managed to grab Dean and our bags; then we set off up London Road towards the roundabout. When we got to Stanley Road we turned left and ran as fast as we could, hearing the police sirens going off in the distance. We didn't stop running until we got to Evington Road, resting outside the Picnic Kebab shop.

'What happened to Tyrone?' I asked Dean, after I'd got my breath back.

'Don't worry about him,' Dean replied. 'I saw him and Simon and the rest running for some cars. They'll be fine. I'll bell him in a bit . . .'

'That was fuckin' crazy,' I said.

'You're telling me,' he replied. 'Come on – we better jet. Them coppers are gonna be looking all over the place.'

'You OK?' I asked him.

'Cool. Might have a few bruises, but that's life.'

'I think I broke Suky's nose,' I admitted.

'That the twat you went through the door with?' asked Dean.

I nodded. 'He's Raji Mann's brother,' I added.

'Great,' replied Dean. 'You know this is gonna lead to more shit, don't you?'

I nodded again.

'Long as we got each other's back,' he said.

'Always, bro,' I told him.

We took a few more breaths and then walked as fast as we could towards home. I spent the entire walk trying to accept that my own cousin had punched me. Even though we'd fallen out, it was the last thing I'd expected. I was part sad and part angry but I tried not to show it, and when we reached Dean's road I told him that I'd call him later. Then I walked home, trying not to get too angry.

SIMRAN

Tyrone looked like he'd been in a fight with a sledge-hammer when I saw him the following Wednesday. I was waiting outside the pool hall for him and when he first walked up to me I thought he was someone else. His left eye was swollen so badly, it was only just open, and he had a bump the size of a golf ball on his forehead. I stood and looked at him and my heart started to pound. Tears welled up in my eyes.

'What happened?' I asked.

'Got in a fight,' he told me, like he wasn't bothered.

'When?'

'At the football.'

I looked into his face to see if he was hiding something from me. He hadn't told me about the fight when he rang me on Sunday to say he couldn't meet up with me that evening. He held my gaze for moment and then looked away.

'You're lying,' I said, hoping that he wouldn't get pissed off with me.

'It was nuttin',' he replied. 'Some Asian bwoi called me some names and I shot it and he kicked me in the head – it happens.'

I gave him a quizzing look. 'What did this lad say?' I asked, although I was sure I knew.

'Just stuff,' he said.

'Racial stuff?'

'Nah – man was just trash talkin' . . . I told you – it happens.'

'But you wouldn't have made a point of saying the lad was Asian unless he had a go at your colour,' I said.

Tyrone smiled. Or at least he tried to.

'You some kind of mind reader?' he asked me.

'Just tell me what he said,' I insisted.

'He called me a monkey, a nigger and a *kalluh*,' he admitted.

I smiled at the way he'd pronounced '*kalah*' even though I was impressed that he knew what it meant.

'It's *kalah*,' I corrected. 'How'd you know what it means?'

'Ain't the first time I've heard it – and anyway, I got me some Asian mates, you know.'

I took his hand and squeezed it. He started to pull away but then stopped. As I stood there, looking at him and feeling sad and guilty and pissed off, all at the same time, a couple of young lads walked past, sniggering when they saw Tyrone's face.

'Yuh get beat up?' asked one. He was wearing a

hoodie with a cap underneath, like some kind of poster boy for an ASBO.

'Fuck off,' snapped Tyrone.

'No need to get wound up, bro,' said the other one. He was wearing drainpipe jeans and Nike Shox that looked like boats. I wanted to ask him where his legs had gone but Tyrone beat me to it.

'Listen, you skinny, no-leg, no-pubes twat – either you can move on or I can give you some of what I got,' he threatened.

'Just askin',' said the first one, looking scared.

'Yeah – sorry, bro,' added the other.

'Just get lost – I'm trying to chat to my girl . . .'

Both of them nodded and then the hooded one smirked. 'She's fine,' he told Tyrone.

For a second I thought Tyrone was going to get angry but he just smiled and shook his head.

'Cheeky likkle raas . . .'

The lads walked away without saying another word, as though the conversation hadn't even happened.

'Little bastards,' Tyrone said, turning to me.

'You do look like a circus freak,' I told him, trying to lighten the mood.

'Oh great! First I get dissed by two kids so young they ain't even started wankin' yet and now my own girl is callin' me ugly.'

'I was only kidding.'

'Hurts, you know,' he told me.

'What – getting ripped by some kids?'

'Nah, man – bruises an' that. There I was, expectin'

some TLC, maybe even some likkle lovin', and what do I get?' he said, pretending to look sad.

'Oh shut up, you big girl,' I replied. 'Like you said – it happens . . .'

Tyrone looked away and then down at the ground and the feeling of guilt that had been stirring inside me came out into the open.

'I'm sorry,' I said, giving him a kiss on the cheek.

He grabbed me round my waist and pulled me closer before he replied. 'What – for being so uncaring?'

'No – because that Asian lad called you names . . . we ain't all like that.'

'Yeah – I know that,' he said, smiling. 'That bwoi was just a knob but you get them everywhere.'

'I suppose you do,' I said, before kissing him.

We drew away from each other, then Tyrone gave me a sly grin and then pulled me even closer.

'Like I said,' he told me with a cheeky glint in his eyes, 'you can find knobs everywhere . . .'

'*Ew!* Get off me, you dirty scutter,' I said, realizing what he was talking about.

But I didn't pull away from him. Instead I kissed him again.

Later on, as we lay on his bed, he asked me whether my family was like the lad who'd called him names.

'You mean racists?' I asked.

'Yeah,' he said, putting his hand under my top and stroking my side.

'Not my actual family,' I told him. 'My mum and dad have got loads of black friends.'

'So what other family is there?' he asked.

I pulled his hand away when it began to stray further north, not because I didn't like it, but because his parents were downstairs.

'My extended family,' I explained. 'It's an Asian thing . . .'

'Like samosas and saris an' that?' he asked, taking the piss.

'You stupid arse,' I said.

'Talking of arses . . .' he said, smiling.

'Oi! I told you – not when your parents are downstairs . . .' I protested, pushing his hand away again.

'Oh – they ain't gonna say nuttin',' he lied.

'Yeah, right – apart from thinking I'm a slag, and that'd be just the impression I'd wanna give them,' I replied sarcastically.

'Never,' he said. 'You're like an angel . . . they'd never think you was a slag.'

'Ah – you're so sweet sometimes,' I said, not meaning it to sound like I was joking: it just came out that way.

'I mean it,' he insisted.

I put my hand to his face and felt a surge of warmth in my belly and the small of my back. 'I know – I wasn't joking,' I said, looking into his beautiful eyes.

'So when do I get to come over to your house and meet your parents?' he asked me.

'Why – you gonna ask for my hand in marriage?' This time I *was* joking.

'You never know,' he said with a smile. 'I might even learn me some of them bhangra moves an' that. Impress yer dad . . .'

'You'd be better off learning all about reggae music, Liverpool FC and funk,' I replied.

'What – your dad into reggae?' he asked, looking shocked.

I nodded. 'Just a bit. He's into soul and that too – anything as long as it's old . . . Anything except bhangra – he don't even allow it in the house.'

'Man sounds cool to me,' he said.

'There's nothing wrong with bhangra,' I protested. 'Some of it's OK – and anyway, my dad's got some reggae tunes that steal bhangra beats . . .'

'Yeah – I heard my old man playing summat the other week that sounded Indian. He said it was some old riddim – the Coolie Skank or some shit,' Tyrone replied, his hands beginning to wander again.

'Oi!'

'Just playin',' he said.

'Well, I better go in a minute – I've got work to do,' I told him.

'Me too,' he said. 'My old man will kill me if I don't get my grades.'

'Maybe they should meet up – your dad and mine, I mean. Sounds like they'd take to each other,' I suggested jokingly.

'Yeah . . . but right now I think you should just hang on for another five minutes . . .'

I tried to protest that I wanted to go, but it would have been a lie and I couldn't be bothered to lie. I pulled him to me and kissed him over and over again.

SIMRAN

Ruby rang me on the morning of the bhangra gig to make sure that our plan was still on. I was doing my usual Saturday morning thing when she rang, sitting in my pyjamas, eating cereal from the box and watching morning telly. When I put the phone down I went back to the sofa, tucked my feet underneath me and continued watching the telly. Five minutes later the phone went again and this time it was Lisa.

'Hey, babe – what you doin'?' she asked me, far too breezily for the time of day.

'Er . . . well, I've just bid my lover goodbye after a night of champagne and dancing and I'm sitting by the pool in my Caribbean hotel. What do you *think* I'm doing?' I asked.

'Ooh – check out sarcastic Simran . . .'

'Well, I'm watching telly. What do you want?'

'You asked me to call you,' protested Lisa.

'When?' I asked, yawning down the phone.

'Text message – last *night*?'

I thought about it for a moment and then remembered sending it. 'Oh yeah . . .' I said.

'Exactly – so don't be giving me grief just because I'm doing something you asked me to do,' she replied, sounding really pissed off.

'I'm sorry,' I told her. 'I'm not awake yet . . .'

'Lucky you,' she said and I realized then that she was upset about something.

'You want me to come round?' I asked her.

'Do what you like,' she said, putting the phone down on me.

I got up and walked into the kitchen, where my mum was messing around with the toaster.

'I'm goin' round Lisa's for a bit,' I told her.

'Already?' she asked, turning the toaster upside down.

A load of burned bits of bread fell out all over the place and she swore.

'She's in a bad mood,' I replied.

'How do you know?' asked my mum, putting the toaster back on the worktop. 'And does anyone ever clean this bloody toaster?'

'She just rang,' I said, answering her first question.

'Oh.'

'And no one cleans a toaster,' I replied to her second.

'Not in this house, obviously,' she said as she looked at the pile of toast crumbs she'd just made. 'So what did she say?' she added.

'Nothing – that's the point,' I told her.

'She put the phone down again?'

'Er . . . yeah.'

My mum looked at me and smiled. 'Well, you'd better be back by twelve,' she insisted. 'You're coming shopping with me.'

'Oh – why can't David go for a change?' I complained.

'Because he's going to be busy,' she replied.

I started to protest but my mum stepped in.

'Cleaning the bathroom and the kitchen,' she said. 'You can always swap.'

'No – that's OK. I love going shopping with you,' I lied.

I went upstairs to get ready, wondering what was up with my best friend.

Lisa opened the door with a little smile and led me through the hallway into the kitchen. She switched on the kettle and then turned to me.

'Sorry,' she said, smiling again.

'You and your putting the phone down.' I grinned. 'It's like throwing your toys out of a pram . . .'

'Yeah – I know. I'm *still* sorry,' she told me.

'You're *always* sorry,' I replied. 'So what's up?'

'Cup of tea?' asked Lisa, ignoring my question.

It took her about an hour of talking rubbish before she decided to tell me what was wrong. It was all about some boy she liked who didn't even know she was alive.

'I've tried everything,' she told me. 'Smiling, charm, even short skirts . . .'

'Which *boy* are we talking about?' I asked.

'I can't say,' she replied. 'I'll tell you some other time . . .'

'And that's what you were all funny about on the phone?'

She nodded.

'Weirdo,' I said.

She shrugged.

'Can I ask you a favour,' I added quickly. 'It's about tonight . . .'

Lisa gave me a funny look and shook her head. 'I'm not going to that bhangra gig – I told you,' she replied.

'I don't want you to,' I said. 'But I do want you to come out tonight.'

The kettle boiled and Lisa took two mugs from a cupboard above the worktop. 'I'm not in the mood,' she replied.

'I know but it might cheer you up and I *really* wanted you to come out with me and Tyrone,' I admitted.

'Like a chaperone?' she joked.

'No – not at all. I just thought you could get to know him a bit more,' I said. 'And besides, he's bringing a friend.'

Lisa gave me a dirty look and put the mugs down. 'Oh *no*! There's no *way* I'm going on a blind date just to help your boyfriend out – you got the wrong chick for that,' she said.

'It's not like that, babe. It's not a *date* – just some mates havin' a laugh.'

Lisa began to make the tea as she replied. 'That's what you said last time – when you wanted to go out with Danny Jones. I ended up with his smelly mate while you were snogging the faces off each other in another row.'

I shrugged. She was talking about a disastrous double

date we'd been on when we were both thirteen. To the cinema.

'He wasn't so bad,' I lied.

'Yeah – apart from the smell of *fish* and the snot that he kept sniffing up his nose. Oh, and the yellow trainers too,' she reminded me.

'At least it was dark,' I joked.

'Not dark enough – those bloody trainers were glowing.'

'You know what your problem is, don't you?'

She threw a couple of tea bags into the mugs before she replied. 'What's that then?'

'You've got no sense of adventure.'

Lisa shrugged. 'I could have done without my sense of smell too on that date.'

'Honestly, it's not a date. I just want you to meet Tyrone properly. *Please* . . .'

'You really like him, don't you?' she asked.

'Yeah – I do.'

She looked into my face. 'But not enough to tell your parents – or even your brother?'

'I wanted you to get to know him first,' I protested.

'Oh,' she said, sounding taken aback.

'And besides – I'm going to tell my family soon anyway.'

'About bloody time too,' said Lisa, handing me a cup of steaming tea with no milk in it. Just how I liked it.

'You got any lemon?' I asked.

'No, you posh cow, I've got lemonade.'

'Not quite the same,' I said, putting the mug down. 'We kind of did something the other night,' I added.

'*Who?*' she asked.

'Me and Tyrone – who'd you think?'

Lisa grinned, put her mug down too and went to shut the kitchen door. 'Oh *yeah* . . . do tell,' she said.

SIMRAN

There were loads of young people milling around in the car park outside the club — most of them couldn't have been much older than us. The crowd was separated along gender lines, with groups of lads eyeing up groups of girls. Some of them were taking crafty slugs from quarter bottles of Bacardi, trying to avoid the doormen who were standing at the entrance, beginning to let people in. When a queue started forming, Ruby, Priti and some other girls they knew joined it. I told my cousin that we'd meet her in the same spot just after one a.m.

'You'd better,' she said, looking worried.

'If I was you, I'd keep an eye out for your brothers — don't worry about me and whether I'm gonna turn up or not.'

'Where are you going anyway?' she asked.

'The Tunnel Bar — Tyrone's dad works there.'

She almost flinched at Tyrone's name and I decided

that I was never going to be an alibi for her again.

'Have fun,' she told me, with an edge to her voice.

I fought back the urge to say something else, something that might have inflamed the situation; instead I walked off to join Lisa, who was talking to some Asian lads. At least, they were trying to talk to her. After we'd left them some way behind us, Lisa swore.

'Immature little shits,' she added.

'Who?'

'Them lads – they were pissed up and one of them asked me if I liked it brown.'

'Liked what brown?' I asked stupidly.

'What do you think?'

'*Ew!*'

Lisa avoided a discarded box of fried chicken and then stepped aside again as another three Asian lads almost walked straight into her.

'Watch where you're going!' she shouted after them.

'Fuck off, you *goreeh* ho!'

I turned and glared at the lad who'd replied.

'You want summat?' he asked.

His mates told him to leave it as I wondered how good he felt, getting aggravated with a couple of girls.

'I bet he's got the smallest penis in the world,' I told Lisa.

'Smaller than that,' she added. 'Come on, let's get to wherever we're going.'

'We'll be there soon,' I said. 'It's only round the next corner.'

She put her arm through mine and we walked on, as I told her about Tyrone's mate.

★ ★ ★

The bar was packed out by midnight but we didn't have to wait to get in. The doormen knew Tyrone, who'd met us outside, and let us in even though there was a queue. Tyrone's dad wasn't around though – he was out with his own mates and Tyrone was pleased about it too.

'Can't be romancin' my gal wit' my dad around, now can I?'

'Why not?' I asked him.

'Nah – that's just embarrassing,' he added, before going off to the bar.

The music was so loud that I had to shout at Lisa, in order to be heard. Tyrone and Azhar came back with some drinks and when Lisa took hers, Azhar leaned closer and spoke into her ear. He had a thin goatee beard and a slightly elongated face, with light brown eyes. And it looked like he'd had his eyebrows plucked. They were just too perfect. He was wearing baggy pants, like the *salwaar* that old Asian women wear, and low-profile trainers that might as well have been slippers. They were yellow. I wondered whether Lisa had seen them and burst into laughter.

'What's so funny?' Tyrone shouted above the music.

'His trainers – and everything else he's got on – *and* the eyebrows,' I admitted.

'He's just flamboyant, that's all. Man always dresses different. Like he's got his own style. Don't take the piss . . .'

'I can't help it. I mean, is that a purse he's got round him?'

I was looking at a small, tan leather thing that was

hanging across his body, to one side. It looked like a girl's accessory.

'Er . . . yeah. I think he got it from Top Shop,' Tyrone replied sheepishly.

'And he's your mate?'

'One of them. He's a lot older than me,' he said.

'I like his shirt though. And his hair,' I added.

The shirt was white with an open collar, and vertical embroidery in white stitching. It was beautiful.

'He's all right, you know – he's just different.'

I watched as he tried to chat Lisa up and she lapped it up like a cat with cream. She was flirting with him for sure but I knew that she was just playing. She'd told me as much when we'd gone to the ladies. I stood on my toes and leaned up towards Tyrone's ear.

'She doesn't fancy him,' I told him.

'No big deal,' he replied.

'Don't you think it's funny though? Watching him trying so hard.'

'I would if I was watching,' Tyrone said. 'But I'm only interested in you . . .'

He put his arms around my waist and gave me a long kiss, as another tune started and the crowd in the bar went mad. Not that I was paying too much attention. I wanted to be somewhere alone with my boyfriend and when he stopped kissing me I leaned against his chest. He smelled great, even through all the cigarette smoke, and his chest felt like someone had carved it out of granite. As I stayed pressed up close to him, I wondered how I was going to tell my mum and dad about our relationship. And that was what it had become. I hadn't been too sure to begin with, but the more time I spent with him, the more I wanted to. He was clever, funny and gorgeous. Perfect. And I was totally into him too, in a way I'd never been with anyone else. All my other boyfriends – all three of them – had been silly crushes that disappeared within a month. This was different though. It felt real and strong and right. I made up my mind that I'd tell my mum first and take it from there.

'I'm gonna talk to my mum in the week,' I told him.

'Because you don't at weekends?' he replied, trying to joke.

'You ain't funny,' I teased. 'I'm gonna talk to her about you and me.'

He raised his eyebrows. 'You sure about that?' he asked, looking concerned.

'Absolutely. If that's OK with you – I don't want you to feel pressured or nothing . . .'

He shrugged. 'Where's the pressure?'

'Because I reckon we've got a good thing here,' I added, hoping that he felt as strongly as I did.

'I know,' he replied. 'You're my first proper girlfriend, you know.'

'What's *proper*?' I asked.

'You *know* . . . proper.'

I kissed him before replying. 'Yeah, I know . . .'

I don't think he heard me say that I loved him because the DJ put on a dancehall tune that was obviously a crowd favourite. A big roar went up and the bass line made the windows vibrate. I didn't mind that he hadn't heard me. I was happy knowing for myself that I loved him. I didn't need anything else. Apart from another kiss.

★ ★ ★

Azhar insisted on walking with us back down to the club where Ruby was waiting. I reckon it was more to do with him fancying Lisa than being a gentleman but I didn't mind. I held Tyrone's hand as we walked and for the first time since we'd met I wasn't worried about who saw us or what they might say. I just didn't care any more. The problem was that others – both strangers and people I knew – *did* care. And that became clear when we arrived outside the bhangra gig, where an even bigger crowd than before was milling about.

We stood by a low wall that surrounded the car park, about ten metres from the club's entrance, waiting for Ruby to come out. I was still holding Tyrone's hand and I noticed that some of the mainly Asian crowd who were hanging around had noticed. A girl wearing a red outfit looked me up and down and then turned up her nose. Her friends whispered something to each other and then gave me dirty looks. I turned to Tyrone and kissed him, trying to wind them up. It worked. The first girl shook her head and called me a whore. Lisa perked up when she heard it.

'What's her problem?' she asked no one in particular.

I watched as she walked over to the girl in red and shoved her in the chest. The girl tried to hold her ground but Lisa is tough, and she towered over her. She grabbed her by the throat and said something to her. The girl's face fell as Lisa let her go and walked back over to us.

'You're *mad*!' laughed Azhar.

'Stupid cow – she deserved it,' replied Lisa.

'So you comin' out again?' asked Azhar, grinning.

'You should watch that,' I replied. 'She's only fifteen.'

'Sixteen in a month,' protested Lisa.

'Yeah, but he's, like, *eighty*,' I joked.

'Lookin' good though,' replied Azhar, striking a pose.

'If you say so,' giggled Lisa.

I looked towards the door just as Ruby made her way out. She was wobbling and looked like she'd drunk far too much. I waited for her to see us but instead she turned to speak to Priti, who'd followed her out. Behind them a load of lads tumbled through the door and I recognized Pally from school. I turned round quickly, hoping that he hadn't seen me. But it was too late.

'Oi, Simran!' he shouted. 'What you doin'?'

He stumbled forward as he spoke and then stood, swaying. He was out of his tree. Tyrone looked at me and then over to Pally.

'Who's that?' he asked.

'Some lad from school. He's a dickhead,' I replied, ignoring Pally.

'*Simran!* Don't ignore me,' Pally said in Punjabi.

'You want me to tell him to get lost?' asked Tyrone.

'No – just *leave* it,' I insisted.

But then Ruby joined us and Pally started getting angry.

'What you standin' with that *kalah* for? Come over here to us real men, sister.'

Tyrone looked at me, shrugged like he was sorry for something and then turned to face Pally. 'You *what*?' he asked, squaring his shoulders.

'I ain't talkin' to you – *bwoi*. I was talking to my sister there,' replied Pally.

'She ain't your sister,' Tyrone told him.

Pally smirked. 'Well, she sure as *fuck* ain't yours, is she?' he said, grinning in that way that really pissed people do when they think they've been really clever.

'She is my girl though,' Tyrone told him.

Pally's face changed from a sneer to confusion and then to anger. He looked at me and spat at the floor. '*What* – you turned me down for a *kalah*? You fucking shot it?' he spat.

I grabbed Tyrone's hand, as Lisa and Azhar stepped towards us. Ruby's face turned crimson.

'Let's go,' I said to Tyrone.

'Nah – he's out of order,' he replied.

'Yeah – the bwoi needs a good slap,' added Azhar, who stepped in front of Tyrone and me. 'You got a problem, kid?' he asked Pally.

'Fuck off, you Paki bastard,' snapped Pally.

Azhar pulled his purse around behind his back and cracked his knuckles. I looked at Lisa with panic in my eyes.

'Stop him!' I urged.

Lisa nodded and pulled Azhar back. '*Leave* it,' she said to him. 'Don't ruin a fun night because of those boys.'

'Come on then!' Pally shouted drunkenly as he swayed on his feet.

'*Leave it!*' snapped Lisa.

Azhar calmed down but he didn't stop looking at Pally. 'I'll catch you next time,' he warned.

'Oh, I'm *so* scared,' sneered Pally before turning his attention back to me.

'Don't look at her,' threatened Tyrone.

Pally ignored him. 'What are you doing – are you some kind of whore?' he asked me in Punjabi.

'I said, don't bother with her,' repeated Tyrone.

'Piss off, you nigger.'

Just as Tyrone stepped forward the doormen threw out a load more Asians, most of them lads I recognized. Desi Posse. My stomach flipped and I grabbed Tyrone's hand.

'Come on!' I insisted. 'That's the rest of his mates. Let's get out of here!'

Tyrone looked at Pally and then at me. 'Just 'cos you're askin',' he told me, anger in his eyes.

I turned and walked quickly back up the street and Tyrone and the rest followed. We didn't stop when Pally shouted after us.

'Everyone's gonna know you're a ho,' he told me. 'Dirty *slag*.'

I ignored him and ensured that Tyrone did the same. We got to the top of the road and Tyrone flagged down a black cab.

'You better get home,' he said, as the cab pulled up to the kerb.

'What *you* gonna do?' I asked him hurriedly.

'Never mind about me and Azhar – we can take care of ourselves,' he replied.

'You *can't* go back to the club,' I told him.

He shook his head. 'Don't worry – I ain't. But that fuckin' bwoi is gonna get it when I see him again,' he spat.

I was about to try and calm him down but I realized that it wouldn't work. He was fuming. Instead I told Ruby and Lisa that we were going.

'You'd *better* take care,' I said to him.

'I will,' he replied, his voice softer this time.

I kissed him and gave him a hug. 'Call me in the morning, OK?'

'Try an' stop me.' He grinned.

I got into the cab feeling less worried, but only slightly. As I turned to face Ruby and Lisa, Ruby gave me a dirty look.

'I *told* you this would happen,' she said.

'*What?*'

'Pally's a nice lad normally. He ain't racist – he wouldn't do that if it didn't bother him . . . I *told* you,' she repeated.

'You know what?' I said to her, my anger rising. 'I don't like you any more. You can lie to your mum on your own from now on.'

She shrugged. 'You'll see,' she replied. 'It ain't right. That *kalah* is gonna get you into big trouble.'

'Why don't you shut your two-faced gob before I shut it for you?' I snapped, meaning it. Ruby looked away.

Lisa whistled softly, a sign that she was embarrassed; then she shrugged and told the driver where we were going. No one spoke on the ride home.

SIMRAN

'You OK?' I asked Tyrone as we came out of the cinema the following evening.

'Nah – that film was lame. I think my brain is meltin'.'

I punched him on the shoulder and called him an arse. 'I meant about last night,' I explained.

'What's the big deal?'

I thought about the nasty things that Pally had said to both of us and realized that it was time to talk about other people's attitudes. I was going to have to deal with them at school anyway so it made sense to talk to my boyfriend about it first.

'The racial stuff,' I said, looking at him.

He nodded towards the pub next to the cinema. 'Come – let's go sit down,' he told me.

I waited on a wooden bench outside as he went to get us drinks. It was eight in the evening but felt earlier and it was a lot warmer than it should have been for the time of year – you could feel the moisture in the atmosphere. There were a few other people outside too, mostly couples like us, either waiting for their films to start or having a drink on the way home. I didn't feel too self-conscious. Tyrone looked like he was in his twenties and most people thought that I looked older than I was. That would have put us in the same age bracket as most of the couples I could see. If we actually were their age, that is.

'Got you lemonade with a twist of lime,' said Tyrone, knocking me out of people-watching.

'Thanks,' I said, stirring the slice of lime around with a straw and watching beads of condensation forming on the outside of the glass. A car engine roared in the car park.

'Thought you might have had enough booze last night,' he added.

'You callin' me a piss-head?' I asked.

'You drank enough.'

I grinned. 'I'm a good Punjabi girl, me. Come from a long line of hard-drinking farmers – it's in my blood.'

'Must be after last night,' said Tyrone, labouring the joke.

'Seriously though,' I replied, 'you sure it didn't bother you – all that stuff?'

'I'd be a liar if I said no,' he told me. 'Them things that bwoi said were harsh an' you ain't even translated what he said to you in Punjabi.'

'Trust me – you don't want to know,' I said.

'Maybe I do.'

'It was like what he said in English. He was calling you names and me a slag,' I admitted.

'I knew I should have smacked that wanker . . .'

I flicked at the straw with a forefinger. 'What would that have done?'

'Dunno, but that's what I felt like doin'.'

'It would have made things ten times worse,' I said. 'And when my uncles and aunts find out about you, their reaction will be bad enough.'

He ran his hand over his head before taking a swig of Coke. 'Is it gonna be that bad?' he asked. 'Because if it is then maybe I ain't worth the grief.'

I gulped when his words began to sink in. Was he trying to get rid of me? I asked him.

'Nah – I don't wanna get rid of you, Simmy. It's just I don't want you to blame me if shit goes wrong with your family.'

'I won't. If they stop talking to me, that's their lookout. How would you be to blame?'

He shrugged. 'I spoke to Azhar about it today. He told me that some Punjabi people don't like blacks – especially the men.'

I raised my left eyebrow. 'What does he know about being Punjabi?' I asked.

'That's where his family are from – the Pakistani side. You really should learn the history of your parents' country,' he said.

'They were both born here,' I corrected him. 'But I know what you mean. My uncles bang on about India and I don't know anything about it.'

'There's elephants,' he replied with a smile. 'And samosas and the *Kama Sutra* . . .'

'Trust you to think about your stomach and sex,' I commented. 'Can't work out the elephants though.'

'I used to love them when I was a kid,' he said.

'*Aaah!*' I said, as stupidly as I could manage.

The couple at the bench next to us gave me a funny look, smiled and went back to their own conversation.

'So, do your uncles and that . . . do they hate black people?' asked Tyrone.

'I dunno – they hate everyone. Put it this way, my brother fell out with a load of my cousins because they called his mate a nigger and other stuff.'

'Your cousins?' he asked.

'Yeah – you know, the biological offspring of my uncles and aunts – you must know the concept . . .'

'Now who's taking the piss?' he said.

'Sorry.'

I drank some of my lemonade as we sat for a while and watched the world go by. Not that there was much of it around on a Sunday evening.

'I know some black people who don't like Asians either,' he admitted.

I sighed. 'I suppose there's people like that in every community.'

'Yeah, but it don't make sense,' said Tyrone. 'I mean, all of us, all us ethnic minority or whatever we're supposed to say – all our people came to this country in the same way . . .'

'I suppose . . .'

Tyrone shook his head. 'Ain't no suppose about it. They was all ex-colonials and they got invited here because there was all these jobs that white people didn't want to do. And they all got the same grief from them skinheads and right-wing politicians,' he continued.

'How come you know so much about it?' I asked.

'I kind of study it,' he said sheepishly, as though it was a big shameful secret or something.

'Really?'

'Yeah – I wanna be a journalist maybe and I'm collecting pictures and stories from my family about when they came over here in the nineteen fifties. I even taped my gramps when he told me about how they used to live when they first arrived.'

In my head another massive tick went on the plus side of my perfect partner chart. Not that there was anything on the other side anyway.

'Can I see it sometime?' I asked, fascinated by what he was telling me.

'Yeah. But like I was saying – mostly our older people had to stick together and that, and now us young ones are messing it up.'

I took his hand. 'Not all of us,' I assured him.

'You know what I mean though,' he said.

'Yeah – I do.'

'And it don't make no sense to me because what's colour all about anyway?'

I nodded. 'I know what you mean.'

'I mean, it ain't like we get to choose what colour we're born. You wasn't sitting in your mum's belly deciding that you wanted to be born Asian or white or whatever – like it's a shopping trip or summat.'

'I've never thought of it like that,' I admitted. 'You're right though . . . and we should really make a move. I've got stuff to get ready for school.'

'Yeah – come on,' he said, downing his drink and standing up.

'But keep talking,' I said to him. 'I'm enjoying it – you haven't mentioned football or looked at my chest once.'

'Cheeky cow.'

I punched him on the shoulder.

Leicester Market,
November 1979

Gulbir Singh told his son to go to the van and open it up. He watched Mandip walk off with his friend Ali in tow, and then turned to his stall, beginning to remove the stock, leaving it in piles on the bench. Once he had piled it all up he climbed onto the bench and began to dismantle the cold metal poles that made up the stall, trying to ignore the fact that his hands were nearly frozen solid.

Darkness had begun to fall and Gulbir wanted to get away before the football fans began to return to the city centre in even greater numbers than they were already. Leicester City had lost heavily and there was a sense of danger in the air. Every now and then Gulbir heard shouts go up and police sirens wail. He took down the top row of poles and then started on the second tier. From his position he could see the black man, Selwyn, beginning to close down his record stall, although he was still playing music. Three of his friends stood around with him, talking and stamping their feet to keep out the cold. He nodded at Selwyn when their eyes met and Selwyn nodded in return.

From his right, past the stalls, out on the street where he had parked his battered old van, Gulbir heard a football chant go up. He turned quickly to see three skinheads walking down the aisle between the stalls, kicking at things and pulling stock from stalls, throwing it to the ground. Gulbir felt himself tense up and searched frantically for Mandip. But he couldn't see his son anywhere, or Ali.

'We've got trouble,' Mr Abbas called from across the aisle.

Gulbir nodded and jumped down from the bench, looking for his hockey stick. But he couldn't see it, buried as it was underneath the stock. He looked around and saw the weary looks on the faces of the other stallholders nearby. Thinking that he might be able to ignore the skinheads, Gulbir continued dismantling his stall.

'Oi, Abdul!' he heard one of the skins shout.

Gulbir turned to see a tall, broad-shouldered skinhead sneering at him, a spider's-web tattoo crawling up the left side of his neck onto the lower part of his jaw. Gulbir felt his fists clench.

'Yeah, you – what you got for me?' continued the skin, as his two friends began to grab at Gulbir's stock and throw it around.

Gulbir tried to stop them but the big skinhead with the

tattoo pushed him to one side. He looked up and saw Mr Abbas approaching with his cricket bat. The skinhead turned, saw Mr Abbas and let out a laugh.

'What's this then – a Paki army?' he sneered.

'Do you want us to do him?' asked one of the other skins.

'Looks like he wants it,' said the tattooed skinhead.

Gulbir waited until he spoke before shoving him with his shoulder. The skinhead, taken by surprise, lost his footing and stumbled sideways a few feet. Once he'd regained his balance he turned to Gulbir.

'You should have got a return ticket back to bongo-bongo land,' he told him. 'Now I'm gonna do me duty as an Englishman and send you back in a box . . .'

Gulbir readied himself but the three skins jumped in as one, throwing wild punches and kicks. Gulbir fell to one knee and raised his arms to protect his face and head. He felt a blow to his ribs and then another; a kick to his back. He groaned, waiting for the rest of the beating, catching a glimpse of one of the skins fighting with Mr Abbas. And then he heard them.

'*Wha' de bumboclaat!*'

He looked up and saw the three black men who'd been standing by the stall running towards him. One of the men lost his woolly hat and his hair escaped, like a nest of snakes swarming and dancing around his head. Gulbir stayed on one knee as he watched the three black men jump the skins and give them a beating. When he was free of blows, Gulbir got to his feet and joined in, along with a few more of the stallholders. Selwyn ran over too, helping Mr Abbas up, blood pouring from a cut to his forehead.

★ ★ ★

When Mandip and Ali ran after the police, back towards their fathers' stalls, they found three badly beaten skinheads lying on the floor, bleeding, and both their fathers arguing with the police. The three Rastamen that Mandip had seen hanging around all afternoon were handcuffed and being led to a police van, struggling all the way – so much so that it was taking three police to one man to get them into the van. Mandip ran to his dad and asked if he was OK. The police, satisfied that they had sorted things out, were now helping the skinheads to the ambulance that had been called for them.

Gulbir looked down at his son as one of the policemen made a comment about Mr Abbas, calling him a 'lucky black bastard' and not caring who heard.

'I'm fine,' Gulbir said to Mandip, with a sad smile.

Mandip looked around at the mess and began to help pick up all the stock that the skinheads had ruined, wishing that he hadn't been hiding in the van, smoking another cigarette with Ali, when the fight had started.

INDERJIT AND PARMJIT GILL

Inderjit turned his Audi A4 down a side street off Evington Road and pulled over to the kerb. He opened his door, leaned out and threw up.

'Easy, bro,' said his cousin Parmjit. 'You drink too much?'

They'd been to a friend's wedding and spent the entire afternoon and evening drinking lager followed by Bacardi and Coke and eating spicy tandoori chicken and thick, mouth-blistering lamb curry. Inderjit threw up twice more before he could reply.

'That curry messed me up. Weren't the booze . . .' he insisted.

'Want me to drive?' asked Parmjit.

'I think you better.'

Parmjit got out of the passenger side and half walked, half stumbled over to the driver's door. Inderjit slid across the seats, avoiding the gear stick by lifting his legs over it, one at a time, his head spinning at the exertion.

'Good piss-up though,' said Parmjit.

'Yeah, bruv – best I been to in a long time,' agreed his cousin.

'I'll drive to ours – you can sleep it off there,' suggested Parmjit.

'Anything you say,' replied Inderjit. 'I just want a bed.'

'Lightweight – you're goin' on like a white boy.'

'*Theery maa dhi lann*,' said Inderjit, swearing in Punjabi at his cousin's slight on his manhood – telling him his mother had a penis.

Parmjit grinned and pulled away from the kerb as an African man walked past, shaking his head at the puddle of puke they had left behind. Parmjit turned left and left again before making a right back onto Evington Road. He put his foot down and the car sped up, sending his stomach into somersaults. But he held it down and at the bottom of the road, where it forked into two, he went right and on up Evington Lane.

They were halfway along when Parmjit saw someone he recognized out of the corner of his eye. 'What the fuck . . . ?' he asked, turning left and pulling up in Mayflower Road.

'What?' asked Inderjit.

'Di'n't you see that?'

'I wouldn't have asked if I had,' Inderjit pointed out.

'Simran . . .'

'Yeah – so what?'

'Kissing a *kalah*,' added Parmjit.

'Get lost! She ain't no slag.'

Parmjit pulled away from the kerb again and drove around the block. He waited at the end of Baden Road so that they wouldn't be seen, got out of the car and peered round the corner. It was definitely Simran and she was hanging off a tall black lad who looked familiar. Parmjit went back to the car.

'It's definitely her!' he said in Punjabi.

'With a *kalah*?' asked Inderjit, getting angry.

'Not just with him – kissing him up like a fuckin' ho.'

Inderjit started to get out of the car but Parmjit stopped him.

'What you doin'? Let me go—'

'No.'

Inderjit looked at his cousin like he was crazy. 'I ain't sittin' here while one of our sisters brings shame on the family.'

'What you gonna do – beat them up?'

Inderjit didn't reply but Parmjit knew what his answer would be.

'Let's just get home and tell my dad,' Parmjit suggested instead. 'And then see how *her* dad reacts.'

'But—'

'No. If we batter dem on the street, people gonna come watch and everyone will know our business, you get me? Best we deal with it cleverer than that,' said Parmjit.

'I ain't dealing wit' nuttin' clever – believe that!' spat Inderjit. 'No *kalah* is going to ruin one of our women.'

Parmjit held his cousin back again. 'I don't see her complainin',' he replied.

'Fine – but drive by 'em again so I know what that *kalah* bastard looks like,' said Inderjit.

Parmjit waited a moment or two before turning left and driving past the couple. They were too busy kissing to see the Audi pass by slowly.

'That's that *kalah* from football!' said Inderjit.

'Yeah, I know,' replied Parmjit. 'He's David's mate.'

'You mean David lets his own sister get touch up by a nigger? *Nah . . .*'

Parmjit sped off, eager to get back home to tell his old man. If anyone knew how to deal with Simran and the rest of her mash-up family, it would be his dad.

'You better pull over,' said Inderjit. 'I'm gonna be sick again.'

'I told you it was too much booze.'

'Ain't the booze,' said Inderjit, as the car slowed to a halt. 'It's the thought of that dirty, banana-eatin' wanker with his hands all over our cousin.'

Parmjit felt a wave of anger as Inderjit spelled out what they'd just seen.

SIMRAN

My parents were waiting for me when I got home. As soon as I walked in the door I knew that something was up. Jay saw me come in, rolled his eyes and told me that I was in for it.

'What?' I asked, still on a high from being with Tyrone.

'You'll see,' he said, running off upstairs.

I went up to my room, hung my coat up and got changed into my pyjamas. When I got back down to the living room, my parents and my brother were sitting in front of the telly, not watching it. I walked in, said hello and sat down next to my dad.

'Have you been hiding something from us?' asked my mum.

'What?'

'Hiding something. Some*one* . . .'

My heart missed about five beats and then started to pound and I got that sinking feeling in my stomach that you get when you know things are going wrong. How the hell had they found out before I could tell them?

'Er . . .'

That was all that came out. My mum glanced at my dad, who turned his head to look at me.

'Someone like a boyfriend maybe?' he said to me, although he had no need to spell it out. I knew exactly what they were talking about. I just didn't get how they knew about it. That was my next question.

'Uncle Rajbir rang about half an hour ago,' David told me. 'He was havin' a go at *me*. Apparently I know who he is—'

'*What?* That's just stupid. How would you know who he is when I haven't told you anything about him?' I asked.

It wasn't the cleverest thing to say. Tyrone was well known and my brother might have seen him down at the community centre or in town. Or at the football, as it turned out.

'Parmjit and Inderjit drove past while you were . . . er . . . snogging,' said my dad.

'*Snogging?* What were they doin' – *watching* me?' I asked, getting angry. I mean, what did it have to do with them? I didn't even like them.

'I don't know,' my mum replied. 'And I don't really care. I just wish you had told us first . . .'

'Who is he anyway?' asked David.

'None of your business,' I snapped. 'You never tell me about your girlfriends, do you?'

My dad cleared his throat, like he does when he's embarrassed. 'Your uncle said that he was a black boy,' he said, being all matter-of-fact.

'He is,' I admitted. 'And if you're going to start being all funny about his skin colour then you can all get stuffed—'

'Hang on a minute, Simran,' warned my mum. 'Don't go making this worse than it is. We're not bothered by his colour. Why didn't you tell us?'

'I was going to – this week . . . it's just that I wasn't sure how you'd react—'

'To you having a boyfriend?' asked my dad. 'It's the same as the other boyfriends you've had. At first I want to tear out their throats with my bare hands and eat their livers with marmalade and toast, and then I calm down, accept that you're a teenager and go with the flow – did you think I was going to lynch the poor lad?'

'I dunno,' I mumbled, feeling a bit stupid.

'The problem is that because we didn't know, your father's family are going to make a big deal out of it,' said my mum.

David snorted. 'And because he's *black*,' he added. 'They're a bunch of racist wankers—'

'Keep that language out of this house,' said my mum softly, which was her highest level of warning.

'Sorry,' said David, 'but I'm right. They was all abusing Dean and the others at that cup game.'

'Football?' I asked, as my stomach did somersaults. It couldn't have been a coincidence that Tyrone had ended up looking like a circus freak on the same day. Just couldn't be.

'Yeah – that cup game we had. Dean got loads of shit—'

'*David!*' shouted my mum.

'Soz . . . He got lots of abuse and his cousin got beaten up . . . and Parmjit and them were all involved.'

My dad gave David a funny look. 'Is that the real reason you don't want to play on their team?' he asked.

'Yeah,' replied David.

'Forget about that,' I said. 'This cousin — what's his name?'

'Tyrone — why?'

'Oh fuck . . .' I said.

My mum glared at me, anger in her eyes.

'Oh, so only you're allowed to swear when you're angry?' asked David.

'What's the big deal, Simmy?' asked my dad, as David started to catch on.

'It's him, isn't it — Tyrone?' he said to me.

I nodded. My mum and dad looked confused.

'Your new boyfriend is Dean's *cousin*?' asked my mum.

'It's looking that way,' I told her.

David told us that he was going to call Dean and find out for sure but then he asked me to describe Tyrone. When I did he just sat there and nodded his head

'It's the same person,' he said. 'But I'm still gonna call Dean.'

I looked at my dad and tried to smile but, even though I couldn't see myself, I know it came out all wrong.

'You don't mind, do you — *really*?' I asked him.

He moved closer and ruffled my hair like he used to do when I was four. 'If I had my way you'd be locked in a room until you're twenty-one,' he joked. 'No — of course I don't mind . . .'

'What about the rest of the family – you know what they're like,' I added.

'Yeah – don't I just. We'll just have to deal with it,' he told me.

'Great,' said my mum. 'That'll be fun . . .'

'So do we get to meet this mysterious boyfriend or not?' asked my dad.

'We'll see,' I replied, jumping up out of the sofa. 'I'm off to do some homework.'

My parents said goodnight and I left the room, feeling much happier than when I'd entered it, although still a little guilty about not telling them myself. I thought about calling Tyrone to tell him but decided against it. I called Paula instead.

DAVID

In the end I went round to Dean's because the credit on my phone was low and Simran was hogging the house phone. His dad said he was in his room but told me that I couldn't stay for long. Dean was behind with a load of work and his dad wanted him to get it finished. He sounded like a carbon copy of my dad. It was no wonder they were so close. Dean opened the door and gave me a funny look.

'You *again*?' he said, smirking. 'You might as well move in.'

'Anything for your mum's cooking,' I said with a grin.

'What's so important that it couldn't wait until the morning?' asked Dean.

I shrugged as I went and sat at his desk, watching the screensaver on his PC. The machine was identical to mine because our dads had got them from the same dodgy bloke down the pub. But Dean's screensaver was different to mine.

On his, a semi-naked woman in a bikini walked across the screen every few seconds, pretending to remove her top.

'I bet your mum ain't seen this,' I said to him.

'Nah – me dad has though. He loves it.'

'Does she actually get her tits out?' I asked.

Dean shook his head. 'Nah – but I got plenty of sites I could show you – if that's what you're after,' he said.

'Don't be a knob, D,' I told him. 'I ain't come round 'cos I need wank material . . .'

Dean grinned. 'Could have fooled me, blood. When was the last time you had a girl?' he asked, taking the piss.

'Your cousin – that Tyrone . . .' I began.

'What about him?' replied Dean, sitting down on his bed and leaning back against the poster above it, so that the footballer in the picture looked like he was running on Dean's head.

'*He's* gotta girl . . .' I told him.

Dean raised an eyebrow. 'What are you – his *keeper*? So what?' he asked.

'Did you know?'

'Know *what*?'

I turned in the chair to look at him. 'That yer cousin had a girl . . .?'

Dean scratched his head. 'You been smoking that homegrown shit from Dutty Dominic?' he asked, talking about a dealer we knew.

'No – I ain't . . .' I told him.

'Well, you been getting' high on summat. What the fuck are you on about?'

I looked him in the eye and wondered if he was hiding something. Not that I was too bothered. But if he did know about my sister and Tyrone, I would have wanted him to tell me.

'He's checkin' my sister,' I told him.

Dean's eyes didn't leave mine for even a split second. 'You *what*?' he said, surprised.

'Simmy and Tyrone – she just told us.'

'*Get lost!*'

I shrugged. 'Some of my family seen them together and told my dad,' I admitted.

'They told your *dad* – about what?'

I looked away for a second or two. 'That she was seein' a black lad,' I continued.

Dean shifted his position so that the footballer was running off the side of his head. 'They the same wankers that was at that game?' he asked.

'Yep . . .'

'And I guess they don't want your sister goin' out with no *kalah*?' he added, using one of the many Punjabi words I had taught him over the years.

'Exactly – they went a bit mad . . .'

Dean looked at me and then stood up. 'Is *that* why you was askin' if I knew anything?' he said.

'Nah – I just wondered . . . I'm not bothered if you did know,' I replied.

He shook his head. 'I would have told you first, bro.'

I nodded. 'Yeah, I know.'

'So why ask?' he said.

I shrugged. 'Dunno.' I didn't have a clue why I'd asked.

'So, your old man cool with it?'

'Yeah – totally. He ain't exactly short of black people he can call friends, is he?' I pointed out.

'Yeah,' said Dean, 'but this is his daughter we're on about. Ain't the same thing . . .'

I got up from the chair and went and stood by his window. 'Depends on what he's like,' I said.

'Who – your dad?'

I shook my head. 'No – your cousin,' I told him.

Dean shifted again and then gave me a funny look. 'That why you're here – to ask me about Tyrone?'

I shook my head. I didn't know why I was there at all. I wanted to know about Tyrone but I'd already met him and I liked him. It wasn't even that I was shocked or nothing. I didn't mind who my sister went out with, as long as they were nice to her. But maybe in my head, right at the back where I didn't notice it, maybe there was some prejudice or something that made me want to check out Tyrone's credentials. I didn't know.

'*Well* . . . ?' asked Dean.

'Yeah – I suppose,' I admitted. 'I mean – I like Tyrone . . . I just wanted your opinion, I think. I don't really know . . .'

Dean looked at me for while and then he stood up too. 'Come on,' he told me. 'My dad's got this really nice French coffee in – I'm gonna have some.'

'You'll be up all night,' I said.

'With all the work I got, I'm gonna need to be,' he replied.

As I followed him downstairs, I shook my head at the way he'd left his work until the last minute again. I was relieved that I hadn't pissed him off, and after he'd made drinks for us and his parents, we went and sat in his living room and he told me all about Tyrone. At one point his mum and Paula, his sister, came in and heard Tyrone's name.

'What's he done now?' asked Dean's mum.

'Chatted up my sister,' I told her.

'*Huh?*'

'Tyrone's goin' out with Simmy,' said Dean.

'He's a lucky boy,' said Mrs Ricketts.

'Oh, so you know then?' asked Paula with a grin.

We all turned to her.

'You *knew*?' I asked.

'*Yeah!* Me and Simmy talk about everything,' she told me. 'She's just called me to say you were coming round.'

'An' you never thought to say nuttin'?' asked Dean.

Paula shook her head. 'Nothing to do with you,' she told him. 'Besides, Simmy made me promise . . .'

'Oh, right,' I said.

'He's a really nice lad,' added Paula.

'Yeah – I was just reassuring David here that Tyrone wasn't a drug dealer or nuttin' like that,' said Dean, winking at her.

I looked at him and then away, as his mum smiled and told me that I had to go soon. I nodded, wondering whether Dean had made his last remark to let me know that he *was* pissed off; or whether it was the kind of joke that he would make. In the end I stopped thinking about it. I would have got paranoid otherwise. I left a few minutes later, telling Dean that I'd catch up with him at school. He just nodded at me in reply.

SIMRAN

If I thought things were going to get better once I'd told my family about Tyrone, I was wrong. The following weekend, early on Saturday morning, my dad's brothers arrived at our house unannounced. I was still in bed, trying to think of a reason for not getting on with all the housework my mum had given me, when the doorbell rang. I thought it was the postman delivering a package and ignored it, but then I heard my mum speaking in Punjabi. I sat up in my bed so quickly that I felt dizzy. Once my head had calmed down I walked over to my bedroom door and opened it. The other voice I could hear was my aunt Pritam's – Uncle Malkit's wife. I walked to the top of the stairs and looked down into the hallway. My aunt saw me and as soon as our eyes met she looked away. I called down to my mum.

'What's going on?' I asked.

'Nothing,' replied my mum, in a tone of voice that said something was definitely up.

'You want me to come down?'

'Get dressed first,' she told me before leading my aunt into the living room.

While I was in the bathroom cleaning my teeth, I heard the doorbell go three more times. Each time my stomach flipped and I began to get worried about what was happening downstairs. I spent as long as I could getting dressed before heading down to the kitchen. David and my mum were in there, standing in front of the cooker.

'What's going on?' I asked for the second time that morning.

'Gill Enterprises,' replied my brother.

'Huh?'

'Your father's family are here – to try and salvage the *bad situation*, as your eldest aunt put it,' said my mum, mimicking my aunt's accent.

I looked at my brother, not understanding.

'God – you can be so thick sometimes, Sim. They're here to talk about you and your unsuitable boyfriend,' he told me.

'Are you havin' a laugh?' I snapped.

'Don't get pissed off with him,' countered my mum. 'It's not his fault—'

'Are you saying it's mine?' I asked quickly.

'No – of course not. You know what they're like . . .'

'Yeah, but why do we have to put up with it?'

My mum shrugged and continued making tea – just the way my dad's family liked it.

'Well, if they give me any shit they can all fuck off,' I said, getting angry.

'I know you're upset but I won't have that language,' warned my mum.

'Sorry,' I said, realizing that it was important to keep her on my side. 'So who's here exactly?'

David grinned. 'Uncle Malkit, Aunt Pritam, Uncle Rajbir and Aunt Jagwant. The Prime Minister, the Pope . . .' He winked at me.

'It's not funny, David,' I told him.

'Is from where I'm standing,' he replied, before feeling sorry for me. 'Just ignore them, Sim. I'm on your side . . .'

My mum nudged him in the ribs.

'And Mum and Dad,' he added quickly. 'And Jay would be too only he's playing on his console.'

'Great!' I sighed.

'You don't have to go in there,' suggested my mum. 'You could always stay out of the way.'

'*Why?* I haven't done anything wrong. Why should I let those idiots win?'

My mum shrugged and told me that if that was the case I should finish making their tea. 'You can say hello when you bring it in,' she said, before going back into the living room.

'I don't believe this,' I told my brother.

'It's proper serious in there,' he replied. 'When I opened the door to Uncle Rajbir, I thought someone was dead. He looked like someone had emptied his bank account . . .'

'Someone *is* dead,' I half joked. 'Me.'

★ ★ ★

When I took in the tea no one spoke to me apart from my dad. In fact none of his family even looked at me except Uncle Malkit, and he gave me the kind of look that someone would reserve for dog shit on their toast. I set the tea down without breaking his gaze and then I smiled sweetly and said hello in Punjabi. That took him by surprise and he had to reply so as not to look like the idiot he was. But even then it was the quickest and quietest of hellos, mumbled through almost closed lips. I looked around the room at the others and none of them responded. I thought about making an exit but in the end I decided to wind them up and stay put. I walked across to where my mum sat on a dining chair and knelt down at her feet.

Aunt Pritam looked down her nose at me, shifting in her seat. I wanted to burst into laughter because this aunt was wearing a shell suit too, a green one. I wondered whether it was a Gill family uniform.

'You *could* get some biscuits,' said my dad, obviously embarrassed.

'And miss all the *fun*?' I replied.

Aunt Jagwant snorted and started talking to Pritam in Punjabi. They were talking about how I was disrespectful and what did my dad expect when I'd been allowed to behave like a white girl from when I was a baby.

'I am *here*, you know,' I told them.

'This is not your concern,' replied Uncle Rajbir, shifting position so that his belly stuck out even more than usual. I looked at his balding head rather than into his eyes.

'They are talking about *me*, aren't they?' I asked.

'Don't cheek your elders!' snapped Uncle Malkit.

'Oh, go and stick your head up your fat ar—' I began but my mum cut me off.

'Go and do that housework,' she told me.

'But—'

'Simran . . .' she warned.

I stood up and stormed out of the room, angry with everyone in it. How could they talk about me when I wasn't going to be there? I wasn't a kid. I walked into the kitchen and slammed the door. David just shook his head at me and lifted his right forefinger to his lips.

'*Ssh!*'

'What?'

'You wanna hear what they got to say?' he asked.

'Yeah – course I do . . .'

'Well, stop being a brat and come and listen,' he said, pointing to the wall.

'What are you on about?' I asked, worried about him. How were we supposed to hear anything through a brick wall?

David must have guessed what I was thinking because he tapped a part of the wall. 'The hatch that Dad blocked up,' he said.

A few years earlier my dad had filled in a hatch that had connected the kitchen and the living room. He'd complained for ages about the smell of curry seeping into the house. But instead of bricking up the hole, he'd just put two old bits of plasterboard across the gap and it was hollow. I looked at David and thanked God that he wasn't as stupid as I was.

'Now shut up so we can hear them,' he told me as I joined him.

My dad's family spent about two hours talking about me and Tyrone and how I'd brought shame on the family name and reputation. I could make out most of what they said but I did miss a few things too. Mostly they complained about what 'other people' would say, meaning the rest of the Punjabi community. Uncle Malkit told my dad that my grandad was distraught and that the family's *izzat* or honour was being dragged through the dirt. Black people weren't like us, I heard him say, and the shame of having a daughter of our family cavorting with a black man was beyond tolerance. It had to stop and my uncle warned my dad that unless he stopped it, the rest of the family would have to do it for him.

When I heard that my heart sank and I started to get really worried about what they intended to do. I'd heard all kinds of stories about so-called honour killings in the media, and more importantly, I was worried about what might happen between my family and Tyrone. But eventually I calmed down, telling myself that I wasn't living in India. What could they do? As it turned out, I should have heard the alarm bells ringing louder than I did because things were going to take a turn for the worse and there was very little that I could do about it. I didn't realize it at the time but I was going to become a victim of my own family's prejudices.

SIMRAN

It started at school the following week. Ruby didn't turn up until Wednesday after another mysterious bout of illness. On the Monday I asked Priti about it because Ruby hadn't answered any of my calls or text messages. I was still upset with my cousin but I don't hold grudges so I thought that we could start to make things up. Some chance. Priti just shrugged when I spoke to her and said that Ruby was under the weather. I tried to find out more, but she interrupted me mid-sentence to tell me that she was in a hurry and walked off, leaving me standing in the corridor.

When I did see Ruby at lunch time on the Wednesday she totally ignored me. So much for trying to be nice. We were at opposite ends of the dining hall. I was standing with Lisa and another girl called Dawn in the queue for food. Ruby had finished her lunch and was talking to Priti and two other Asian girls. When our eyes met, I smiled and waved but Ruby turned away and started talking to one of the other girls, Parminder. I nudged Lisa.

'She just blatantly ignored me,' I said.

Lisa asked me who I was on about.

'Ruby . . .'

'Really?' she replied, looking surprised.

'Just now . . .' I said.

'You must be mistaken – why would she ignore you?'

'I dunno. But I'm about to go and find out . . .'

I left the queue and walked over to my cousin, who had her back to me and couldn't see me coming. Parminder, the girl she was chatting with, did see me though and she told Ruby. My cousin turned round just as I reached her.

'What's your problem?' I asked.

Ruby couldn't look me in the eye. 'Nothing,' she said lamely.

'Must be something because you just ignored me. Blatantly . . .'

She looked at her friends and then down at the floor.

'Don't look at them – they're not the ones with the problem,' I said, getting angry.

'I can't—' she began, only for Parminder to butt in.

'She don't wanna talk to you, you slag,' she snarled, like the dog that she was.

'You what?'

'You heard me, you dirty bitch,' said Parminder.

My anger subsided because I was so shocked at what she'd just called me. That, and the fact that neither Ruby nor Priti defended me. They just stood where they were and said nothing.

'So you can get back to your *goreeh* mates and that monkey you call a boyfriend,' continued Parminder.

I wanted to slap her but I couldn't. Instead I turned on my heels and walked back to Lisa, feeling helpless.

'How can she just walk around with no shame?' I heard Parminder ask after me. 'Like she ain't doing nothing wrong . . .'

By the time I reached Lisa, I had tears in my eyes.

'What happened to you?' she asked.

'Nothing,' I said, like a little girl.

'So why are you crying?' She looked concerned and angry in equal measure.

'Just forget it . . .' I said, wiping my eyes.

'Forget it?' she asked. 'What did they say to you?'

'They called me a dirty bitch,' I said, more tears replacing the first ones.

Lisa slammed her tray down on the counter, making a couple of Year Seven girls jump in fright. 'Fuck this!' she snapped, heading off to confront Ruby and her friends.

I wanted to follow her but I couldn't. Instead I just stood where I was and watched as Lisa argued with Parminder, slapped her face and got herself excluded from school for two days.

I spent the rest of the afternoon avoiding everyone and keeping my head down. I wasn't too worried about Lisa because she wasn't the kind of person who got into trouble regularly, and our school excluded people in the same way that someone might decide to eat an apple instead of a pear. It was all knee-jerk stuff and I was sure she'd be OK. When school finished I walked out of the main gates and down towards the bus stop on my own, ignoring a few jibes from a couple of Asian lads as I made my way past the car park entrance. They shouted out 'slag' and a few other things in Punjabi, which I'm sure were aimed at me, but I just kept on walking. On the bus I sat on my own, and by the time I got home I was really upset. I sat in my room for ages, crying and then getting angry with myself for being so stupid. I only calmed down when Lisa called me and asked me to go round to her house.

Later that evening I told my mum what had happened and she asked me if I wanted her to call Ruby's mum and have a go.

'What's the point?' I said, shaking my head. 'Ruby's obviously decided to side with all the other arseholes . . .'

'I'm surprised she reacted the way she did,' replied my mum.

'I'm not – I kind of asked her about it a few weeks ago and she told me that I was stupid for even thinking about going out with Tyrone.'

'Oh – you spoke to her before you spoke to me?' she asked.

'Yeah – course I did . . . I thought she was my friend,' I replied, getting all tearful again.

'It really bothers you, doesn't it?' said my mum, putting her arm around me.

I nodded. 'We've been friends since we were little,' I told her, as if she needed reminding. 'I mean – we're not just cousins . . .'

'I know, Simmy,' said my mum. 'She'll come round in

the end. And who's to say that you'll be with Tyrone a year from now?'

I looked at my mum and felt myself getting angry. Was she trying to put me off him too?

'It's not about how long I'm with him,' I insisted. 'It's about why there's all this pressure just because he's black. I don't want to be the kind of person that does that – judges people because of their skin . . .'

My mum shook her head. 'I wasn't trying to put a dampener on things, sweetheart,' she replied. 'I was just pointing out that teenage romances can sometimes seem like the only thing that matters, but people grow up . . .'

'Like you and Dad did?' I asked, in an unfriendly tone.

'OK,' she said, 'I get your point.'

'She can rot in hell.'

'Who?' asked my mum.

'Ruby – if she wants to be funny with me then I don't care,' I said.

'You obviously do,' argued my mum. 'It wouldn't hurt as much otherwise.'

'Stuff her.'

It was Priti who told me the truth the following morning. She got the same bus as I did and when she saw me she came over and sat by me. I wasn't in the mood for more shit and I told her so.

'I just wanted to talk to you,' she replied, half smiling.

'You didn't talk yesterday,' I reminded her. 'You didn't say a word when that bitch was having a go at me. Lisa got excluded because of your bitch friend.'

'I'm sorry,' she told me, 'but Lisa did slap her and I'm

not trying to defend Parminder. She's just got her opinion, that's all.'

'So that's fine then, is it? She's got her racist viewpoint and we all have to deal with it?'

Priti shook her head and excused her friend even though she'd just said that she wouldn't. 'She's no racist,' she argued.

'She called Tyrone a monkey – what's that, charm?' I snapped.

'It's just that you seem to think you're different to the rest of us,' she said.

I gave her a dirty look. 'Who *are* "us"?' I asked.

'The other Asian girls at school. You've got your liberal parents and your white mates – it's like you think you're separate from us,' she explained.

'That's just stupid . . .' I replied.

'No it isn't. It's like you're not proud to be Indian or something.'

I shrugged. 'That's because I'm not,' I said.

'So what are you then? 'Cos you ain't white . . .' Priti asked.

'I'm British,' I told her. 'I wasn't born in India so how can I be Indian?'

'You'll always be Indian,' she said, like it was an un-answerable truth.

'No I won't – and anyway, what has that got to do with Ruby ignoring me?' I asked her.

'It's all part of the same thing. Even when we were little you acted like you were white . . . Ruby isn't allowed to talk to you any more.'

I waited for a moment before replying to the two

bombshells she'd decided to drop on my head. 'Firstly, I don't think I'm white — not that there's anything wrong with being white. Secondly, who told Rubes that she isn't allowed to talk to me?'

'Her parents — and her brothers.'

I shook my head. 'I should have known they'd be involved,' I said.

'It's not just about that, Simran. You do think you're better than us. Like how you hang around with Lisa and diss bhangra and all that. And now, with your black boyfriend . . .'

I shook my head again. 'Just get lost,' I told her. 'You think you can slag off Lisa and Tyrone and I'm going to wear it. Well, you're wrong.'

Priti stood up. 'You'll see,' she replied. 'When Lisa and Tyrone have gone or dumped on you — we'll still be here . . .'

'Ain't gonna happen,' I told her.

'Well then, you carry on acting white and hanging around with *kaleh*. See where it gets you.'

I looked at her and smiled sarcastically. 'I will,' I replied. 'See ya!'

Then I turned my head to the window and looked down at the passing traffic. Priti stood where she was for a moment and then walked to the back of the bus, where some of her Asian friends were waiting for her. I heard them say a few things about me but this time I didn't even get angry, never mind upset. I just sat where I was and thought about Tyrone's smile.

DAVID

I didn't know how bad things were for Simran until about two weeks after she'd told us she was seeing Tyrone. I was walking through the dining hall with Dean when I saw her sitting with Lisa. There was a mess on their table and when I walked over to take the piss I saw tears in my sister's eyes. I looked at Dean, who saw that I was angry and rubbed his head, something he always did when he could see trouble brewing. I turned back to Simran.

'What happened?' I asked her.

'*Nothing . . .*'

I looked at Lisa. '*Well?*'

'Simran better tell you,' she replied.

I pulled a chair out and sat down next to my sister. 'Tell me,' I insisted. I didn't know why she was crying but I wasn't going to leave it until I found out.

'Some boys were picking on her,' said Lisa.

'*Lisa!*' shouted Simran, getting even more upset.

'*What* boys?' I demanded.

This time my sister heard the edge in my voice and she turned to face me. I put my hand on her cheek and wiped off some tears. Dean sat down next to me.

'Just tell us, sis,' he said to her.

'Pally and his mates,' she blubbed.

'Pally – that skinny wannabe *gangsta*?' I asked, feeling my blood begin to speed up as it went around my body. Simran nodded.

'Why's he picking on *you*?' asked Dean.

In my heart I already knew the reason why.

'It's about her seein' Tyrone,' said Lisa, answering for my sister.

'Is that right?' I asked Simran, who nodded. 'What they been saying?'

'They were calling me names – not just them, some of the girls too. Calling me a slag and a whore . . .' she admitted.

I stood up and turned to Dean. 'You don't have to get involved in this, bro,' I told him. There was trouble brewing and I didn't want my best mate to get caught up because of me.

'Fuck that,' he told me, getting up too. 'That's my cousin, bro. And the last time I let you handle shit on yer own, I had to clean you up after.'

He grinned, finding a joke in a serious situation, like always. I turned to my sister and Lisa.

'Forget about them . . . I'll deal with it,' I told them.

'*We'll* deal wid it,' added Dean.

'Just don't get into no trouble,' said Lisa. 'I got excluded for having a go at one of those girls.'

Dean shook his head. 'Ain't no one gettin' kicked out. We're just gonna have a quiet word – that's all,' he replied.

I looked at him like he was mad. I wasn't in the mood to talk to Pally. I wanted to rip his throat out.

Me and Dean caught up with Pally outside the science block. He was with a couple of his crew and they were sitting talking to a group of girls, including my cousin Ruby. I watched him for a second as he sat on the grass and bragged about his dad letting him drive the family Mercedes. Saw the way that the girls seemed impressed by his shit. Then I nudged Dean.

'Like I said – you ain't gotta get into this,' I told him.

'An' watch my bro get grief all on his own? Ain't happenin',' he replied.

I walked over to Pally and put on a smile. 'Yes, Pally!' I said, acting like he was my best mate.

'Easy, rude bwoi . . .' he replied, grinning. The knob.

I grabbed him by the throat and shoved him back into the ground. His mates jumped up but they didn't do anything. I sat astride him, pinning him to the floor, and leaned down to whisper to him.

'You ever say anything to my sister again – I'm gonna kill you – you get me, rude *bwoi*?'

I spat out the last word. Pally struggled underneath me but I had him pinned down good and in the end he nodded.

'Don't think I'm joking either,' I added. 'Don't *fuck* with my family . . .'

One of his mates made a move towards me but Dean grabbed him and gave him a slap.

'Nah, nah, nah, bad bwoi – best you just leave it,' he told Pally's mate.

The lad didn't move. I reached into the grass and pulled out a big clump with I shoved into Pally's face, and then I slapped him, leaving him on the ground. I stood up and turned to Dean. The girls were all standing too, wide-eyed and scared.

'Let's go,' I said to Dean, who nodded once and followed me back into school. Behind us I heard Pally shout that I was a dead man. I turned round and gestured for him to come to me but he stood his ground, never once looking directly at me.

That evening I knocked on my sister's bedroom door and waited for her to let me in. When she did I saw that she was with Lisa, who was lying back on her bed, wearing a very short skirt. I tried my hardest not to check out her thighs but I couldn't help myself. She was buff.

'Like what you see?' Lisa asked, teasing me.

'Er . . . I weren't . . . er . . .' I stammered, like a dick.

'Course you weren't,' she said to me, as I felt about five centimetres tall.

I decided to get to the point. Fancying your little sister's mate was bad news, no matter how fit she was.

'They won't be bothering you no more,' I said to my sister.

'You didn't do anything stupid, did you?' she asked in reply.

'Nah – just spoke to Pally. He looked like he got the point . . .' I said with a grin.

'Ooh – you're so *tough*,' teased Lisa.

'Shut up!' I replied.

'Charm too! You're real husband material,' she continued.

I ignored her. 'Just tell me if it happens again,' I said to Simran.

She nodded.

'And you,' I said, turning to Lisa, 'you wanna get a longer skirt . . .'

'And spoil the view?' she replied with a big smile. 'Now why would I want to do that?'

I grinned and left.

SIMRAN

The door slammed shut downstairs, making me jump. It was the following Sunday and I was doing some maths revision, trying to get a head start for my exams, which were only a few months away. I heard my mum shout something at Jay and knew they were back from the *gurudwara*. They'd been to a blessing – organized by my mum's best friend. I put my pen down and decided to make myself some tea and find out how it went. My parents would have seen some of my dad's family at the temple and I wanted to make sure that they hadn't said anything else to my dad. Fat chance.

My little brother was already playing on his console by the time I got to the kitchen. He smiled at me when I walked in. My parents weren't in a good mood.

'What's up?' I asked my dad.

He was standing by the fridge, drinking from a can of

Coke. 'Oh – nothing much,' he said, with an edge in his voice.

'Sounds like it,' I replied as I walked over to the kettle, picked it up and filled it with water at the sink.

'We saw your uncle Malkit,' my mum told me. She was leaning against the worktop and she looked angry.

'What have they said now?' I asked.

'You don't want to know,' my dad told me. 'It's our problem.'

I hate it when people say things like that. Of course I'm going to want to know. I switched the kettle on and went and stood next to my mum.

'Was it about me?' I asked.

'You, me, the people at the *gurudwara* – every bloody Punjabi from here to sodding Amritsar – that's who it was about . . .' my dad replied.

'I don't understand.'

'Oh, it was the usual stuff about family honour and how many people think badly of us,' explained my mum.

'Apparently my eldest brother is now the laughing stock at the temple. He's even been asked to resign as treasurer. And on top of that, people are talking about him – *apparently*,' added my dad.

'Oh,' I said, because I didn't know what else to say.

My dad emptied his can and went into the living room. I looked at my mum, who shrugged and told me to leave him alone for a while.

'He's in a really bad mood,' she told me. 'Your uncle really did a job on him.'

'But he knew they'd be like that,' I said.

'Not that bad. Your uncle went for it – talking 'bout your grandad, the family, the job offer . . .'

'What, the sandwich shop thing?' I asked.

My mum nodded.

'That's not fair . . .'

'That's not all, either. Apparently your grandad is so upset he's stopped eating.'

I gulped down air. I hadn't seen him for a while but I loved my grandad. And what my mum was telling me didn't sound like him at all.

'I don't believe it,' I said. 'He wouldn't – he's not like them.'

'That's what your dad said but your uncle insisted.'

'I don't care what he said,' I told her. 'It's not true. I'm going to ring him—'

'You can't . . . Until you stop seeing Tyrone we can't go round or speak to them or anything.'

I glared at my mum, mistakenly thinking that she was telling me to dump my boyfriend. But it wasn't that at all and she took no time to tell me so.

'Don't look at me like that. *I* didn't say that you should stop seeing him. That's what your uncle said.'

'I'm sorry,' I said, feeling stupid for jumping the gun.

'Not half as sorry as your father,' she replied.

'Is he going to side with them now?' I asked.

'It'll be a first if he does,' she told me. 'I think he's just trying to get his head round it, that's all.'

'So you two have talked about it then?'

She nodded. 'In the car on the way home.'

'And . . .?'

She shrugged. 'You'll have to ask your dad that – when he's in a better mood . . .'

I swallowed hard. 'He's going to tell me to dump Tyrone, isn't he?' I said.

'I didn't say that – but you know how much his father means to him. After everything that happened when we got married . . . It's something that he's going to have to give a lot of thought—'

'But he did!' I complained. 'He said it was OK. He told me so.'

'He hadn't been threatened with losing a good job offer then,' she said without any hint of drama.

'I don't believe this!' I snapped, storming off up to my room without my tea.

My dad came up to my room around five p.m. that evening and knocked gently on the door. He called out my name a few times until I eventually told him he could come in. When he walked in he smiled at me but it wasn't a normal, happy smile. There was a hint of sadness behind it. Like he was accepting something bad. That just made me feel even more anxious. He came and sat by me on my bed, and asked me if I was OK. I shook my head.

'Not if you're going to tell me to dump Tyrone,' I told him.

He smiled his sad smile again. 'That's not what I'm asking,' he replied.

I gave him a quizzing look. 'But you *are* asking something . . .'

He nodded.

'And what's that?'

'I dunno,' he admitted. 'I mean, I really don't mind that Tyrone is black – honestly. How could I? It's just that . . .'

'You're gonna end up saying what everyone else has,' I butted in. 'Ruby was all "It's just that . . ." That's the bit where you tell me that we're not the same, Asians and blacks, and start excusing your own racism—'

'No – you've misunderstood what I was going to say,' he insisted. 'I don't think that there's some kind of huge barrier between black people and Asians – I just want to know if you think you're doing the right thing . . .'

I sat up in my bed, angry. 'Right by who?' I asked.

'By you,' he replied, catching me off-guard.

'I really like Tyrone,' I told him, 'more than anyone I've ever met, and I want to be with him. He's clever and he's funny and he always looks after me. Every time he smiles I feel all warm and happy . . .'

My dad nodded along as I spoke.

'So *you* tell me,' I continued. 'Am I doing right by me?'

'Seems that way,' he admitted.

'So what the hell are you *talking* about?' I asked. 'I thought *I* was the teenager here . . .'

That brought out a half-smile, no more, from my dad.

'I guess you're right,' he said. 'I'm not making this very clear, am I?'

I sighed. 'Making *what* clear?' I asked.

'Are you sure you're going to be with him for a while?' he replied.

'How am I supposed to answer that, Dad?'

'I just don't want us to go through all this and then you end up with another crush on someone else—'

'It's *not* a crush,' I said through gritted teeth.

'But do you see what I mean?' he asked. 'Is it a long-term thing or some teenage bit of fun?'

'I haven't got a crystal ball,' I told him. 'How can I know what'll happen next week or next month? All I'm saying is that I like him and I'm going out with him and that's it.'

'It's just that there's a lot to consider – all the tension and the stress,' he pointed out.

'Just like you and Mum had when you were younger,' I said.

'Maybe,' he replied.

'Maybe nothing. It's one rule for you and Mum and another for me—'

'You aren't about to marry him,' said my dad.

'That's not the point. I want to be with him. He's my boyfriend and I'm not dropping him just because your family are giving you shit about it.'

My dad looked away. 'They aren't going to help me out with that shop either,' he said.

I should have stayed calm and tried to think about things from his point of view. I should have tried to empathize. But I couldn't – not at the time. I was too angry. I really thought that he was trying to put doubts in my head about Tyrone, trying to turn me off him, and I resented it. My reaction was bad too.

'I couldn't give a shit about your bloody shop!' I screamed, jumping off my bed.

'Simran – I was only—' he began but I didn't give him a chance.

'*No!* Would we even be *having* this conversation if my boyfriend was *Asian*?'

'Simmy . . .'

I grabbed my jacket and my phone and turned to him. 'You're racist — just like your brothers. You just can't accept it, that's all,' I said, quietly but harshly. Then I ran downstairs and out of the door, not sure where I was going.

I wound up on Evington Road and walked into a fried chicken shop to get myself a drink. As soon as I walked through the door though, I wished that I hadn't. A couple of black girls from school were in there and they both gave me dirty looks. I tried to ignore them but the taller of the two, Misha, bumped into me as I passed her.

'Ain't there enough Paki boys at school?' she sneered, right in my face.

I wanted to get out but I couldn't, so I decided to put on a brave face, maybe because I was still so angry after talking to my dad. Whatever the reason — it was a bad move.

'You what?' I asked, stepping back.

'Why you gotta t'ief the black men too?' she continued. 'The whole school is nearly full up of your kind anyhow . . .'

'Ain't none of your business,' I told her.

'Black men ain't *your* business either,' she said, grabbing me around the throat.

I turned my eyes to the counter but the assistants were all in the back. I could hear them talking and laughing but I couldn't see them. Which meant that *they* couldn't see me either. I tried to struggle free but the other girl, Maya, grabbed me too.

'You best stick to your own kind, you coolie bitch!' Misha spat.

I could feel my heart thumping as I waited to get beaten up, but it didn't happen. Instead I heard Paula's voice, telling the girls to leave me alone. They let go of me, and as I looked up I saw Paula slap Misha hard on the face.

'Now you better leave before I get really angry,' Paula told them.

'What's it gotta do wit' you?' asked Maya.

'That's my sister right there. And her boyfriend is my cousin . . .'

'She ain't your sister,' sneered Misha.

Paula shook her head. 'More than you, she is,' she told them.

The two girls thought about it for a moment but then they left anyway. Paula turned to me and asked me if I was OK. I shook my head and started to cry.

DAVID

Dean told me that we should avoid the community centre for a while, as we sat in my bedroom, just hanging out. My parents were still pissed off after their visit to the *gurudwara* earlier in the day and I wanted to go out for a while. But Dean wasn't having it.

'Them man are all over that place,' he told me, talking about the Desi Posse.

'So?' I asked.

'So why go and step into the vipers' nest, bro?'

I shook my head. 'That place was ours before they got there – why should we take a back seat to them?' I asked.

'Fair enough.' Dean shrugged. 'But if we're goin' down there you best be ready for the consequences.'

'You sound like a teacher,' I told him. 'I ain't running scared of no man.'

Dean grinned. 'So let's go then – besides, there's this girl I wanna chat to – told me she'd be there, you get me?'

I shook my head again. 'All you ever do is think wit' yer balls . . .'

'Is there any other way?' he asked, jumping up.

The Desi Posse were hanging around the entrance to the old warehouse that housed the community centre and the youth club. It was called the Asian Youth Association but non-Asian people weren't excluded from going there. The guys that ran the centre were thinking of changing the name to make it more 'inclusive', as they put it, but some of the Asian lads, especially the DP, thought it belonged just to them. That was the vibe I got as me and Dean walked up.

I saw Pally in the group of five lads and ignored him. I didn't want to get into anything, and besides, the lads were all younger than me and Dean so I didn't think there'd be any trouble. Dean headed up the stairs to the main part of the centre, where he said a couple of girls he knew were waiting.

He grinned at me. ''Bout time we got you a gal anyway.'

I walked in behind him and saw a few more lads at the pool table, all Asian. Dean went over to the girls and started to talk to them. I stood where I was and watched the door and then the lads at the pool table. They were looking in my direction but not looking me in the eye. Something didn't feel right and I decided to go back to the door and see what the lads at the bottom of the stairs were doing. When I looked down the metal stairs I saw Pally on his mobile phone to someone. My head told me not to be paranoid but I was anyway. I had a feeling he was calling for back-up.

I walked over to Dean to tell him what was on my mind, but as soon as I reached him he introduced me to a girl called Kelly. I had to gulp down air when I saw her, she was so fine, and then struggled to say anything. My eyes fixed on her face, which was dark skinned, like her family might be from Sri Lanka or somewhere in southern India. She had the most amazing lips and her eyes kind of shone. It was like someone had smacked me in the mouth with something.

'Hi!' she said with a smile. 'So, are you Dean's mate?'

'Er . . . yeah,' I said, taking a crafty look at her tits. My head went light.

'More like my brother,' added Dean.

'He's better looking than you,' Kelly told him.

'Nah! An' I just introduced you to him,' replied Dean, pretending to be hurt by her words.

'So do you, like . . . go out an' that?' she asked me.

'I suppose so,' I replied, looking at her white shirt and then down to her jeans. Her toenails were painted light green. 'Out where exactly?'

'Bars and clubs and stuff . . . ?' she said.

'Now an' then – why?'

She smiled. 'Next time you go, you could take me,' she told me, all brazen.

'Er . . .'

She got out her mobile and passed it to me. 'Put your number in,' she insisted. 'That way I can call you, can't I?'

I put the number in and then remembered Pally and his mates. I looked around to see what was going on. Nothing had changed but that didn't mean it wouldn't.

'He could be busy though,' Dean told Kelly.

'Oh yeah?'

'Yeah – my bro is what you might call popular, you get me? He might be out with another one of his girls . . .'

Kelly looked me up and down and then shook her head. 'He don't look like he's the type. He looks decent,' she told Dean.

As Dean started banging on about something else, Pally walked through the door with two other lads. They were older than the ones he'd been standing with and one of them was huge. I turned to Dean.

'We got beef,' I told him.

'Huh?'

I nodded towards the door.

'Shit!'

Dean told Kelly and the other girl to step back and then he walked over to the pool table, shoved a lad out of his way and grabbed the pool cue. One of the youth workers, the *wrong* one when it came to stopping fights because he was so skinny, stepped out of a side office and saw what was happening. He strode over to Pally and the two lads and told them to leave as Dean walked back to my side. The huge lad, who was wearing a turban, smacked the youth worker, who went down like a plane without wings. Then he turned and looked at me. Pally stepped up.

'You got anyt'ing you waan say now?' he asked.

'Depends,' I told him, all the time keeping an eye on Mr Turban.

'Think you're a bad man – well, let's see . . .' spat Pally.

Mr Turban stepped towards me, looking all mean, and I took one step to the side. He was going to throw a punch and I was ready. When he did, it was obvious and slow, so

I ducked it and brought my left fist up under his chin. He wobbled a bit but stayed up. Not for long though. Pally's face dropped as Dean smashed the cue against Mr Turban's head a few times and he hit the ground, out cold. I saw him drop and turned to Pally, charging at him. We fell towards the door, just as Raji Mann was coming through it. I felt a punch on the back of my head as I fell. I hit the ground, span to one side and jumped to my feet, turning to see Dean and Raji trading punches. They'd hated each other since we were all in primary school and Dean was getting the better of Raji.

Then I felt a sharp pain in my side. Pally had grabbed the cue and stabbed at me with it. He swung it at my head. I put up my arm and heard a loud crack. Thinking it was my arm, I pulled back, quickly realizing that it was the cue that had snapped. Pally stepped in and threw a couple of punches and that's when I really went mad, punching the left side of his head and face over and over, until my hand seemed like a blur. When I stopped, Pally's face was already puffing up and his eyelid was cut. He was crying.

Someone else grabbed me from behind, a strong grip that I couldn't shake off. When I turned my head I realized it was two more of the men that ran the place, only these two, Gary and Patrick, were rough. I relaxed as soon as I saw that Patrick had me, and even when he threw me to the ground, I didn't complain. I didn't have a death wish. Instead I looked towards Dean and Raji, who were being held at arm's length by Gary. Raji looked at me.

'Keep hidin' behind these *kaleh*!' he spat at me.

'*Yeah?*' I shouted back, standing up.

Patrick stepped towards me, a warning in his eyes, and I held up my hands in surrender.

'Every Desi is gonna know about this,' continued Raji. 'Every taxi driver an' shop owner and bad bwoi . . . !'

Gary told Raji to shut up, only to get a mouthful of racist abuse, which he didn't take too kindly to. He span Raji round in one movement and then bundled him out of the door. Raji's head hit the door and the doorframe on the way out, something that Gary made sure of. When he came back in he was fuming and he turned to Pally, who shook his head and then made a quick exit.

'Thanks, Patrick,' I said, as I calmed down.

Patrick gave me a dirty look. 'Thanks? I should kick your fuckin' teet' out a yer head . . .'

'But,' said Dean, 'they started it.'

'I don't care. You're all barred,' Gary told him.

'But that ain't—' I began.

'Until you can keep your shit to yourselves, you ain't welcome here,' Gary said to me.

'And the next time we hear that *kalah* shit,' warned Patrick, 'this place is getting shut down. We ain't here to get abused.'

'But that ain't us . . .' said Dean.

'I couldn't give a *raas*,' replied Patrick, as Mr Turban finally began to stir.

Patrick looked at him, then turned to the youth worker who'd been knocked out and was now swaying on his feet. 'This the one that smacked you, Kev?' he asked.

Kev nodded. Patrick looked down, spat and then kicked Mr Turban in the head. He went down again.

'Best call the police then,' Patrick told Kev.

SIMRAN

Paula walked me to Tyrone's house and when he opened the door she told him what had happened. He shook his head as we sat in his parents' living room.

'Wait till I see them two,' he said angrily.

'Forget about it,' Paula told him. 'They're just stupid.'

'You OK?' he asked me.

I shook my head. 'No,' I told him. 'It's not just this. I'm getting shit from my family too.'

'What — from your parents?' he asked. 'I thought they were OK with it?'

'Not them — but from my uncles and cousins. And then there's all those people at school.'

I'd told him about David's run-in with Pally and about all the abuse I'd had from the Desi Posse. He'd reacted badly at first but in the end I'd calmed him down. Now he was getting angry all over again.

'I'm gonna have to deal with them,' he told us.

'It's just the same shit, over and over again,' I said. 'Why can't they just leave us alone?'

Paula sighed. 'You knew it would be hard,' she told us both.

'Why did we?' asked Tyrone.

'Oh come on, Ty. Did you really think it was going to be like a normal relationship?'

'Yeah – I did,' he replied. 'I don't get why it's a big deal . . .'

'Then you're naïve,' she said. 'Some people are just too prejudiced to let it go.'

'You sound like my mum,' I told her, realizing that we'd had this conversation already.

She smiled. 'And your mum is right, as usual. It's not your fault – it's just the way some people are . . . How many black/Asian couples you ever seen?'

I shrugged. 'I saw one in the supermarket,' I replied, although Paula already knew that.

'How many others?' she insisted.

'Not many,' admitted Tyrone.

'Exactly. It's like breaking new ground,' she told us. 'There's bound to be problems.'

'But should we just forget about it then?' I asked, as Tyrone gave me a worried glance. 'Just let the idiots win?'

'No – you should stick to your guns,' Paula replied.

'Despite all the shit?'

'Yeah – if you two really want to be together – if it's not just some passing thing . . .'

When she said that I thought about my dad and how angry I'd got when he'd said the same thing. That was when I realized that I'd been wrong to judge him so quickly. I turned to Tyrone and smiled at him.

'Well?' I asked. 'Do you really want to be with me?'

'Yes,' he told me. 'What about you?'

I smiled again. 'You know I do . . .' I went over and gave him a kiss and then sat in his lap.

'In that case' – Paula grinned – 'you need to be honest and realize that things will happen that piss you off.'

'OK,' I said, nestling my head against Tyrone's chest.

'Although I still can't understand why you'd want to go out with Ty,' added Paula. 'He's always been a little shit . . .'

'At least I never set fire to my own hair,' he replied.

'Oh yeah,' I said, remembering when Paula had put too much hairspray on and then leaned over the cooker to light a gas ring with a match.

'That ain't funny, you know,' she said seriously. 'I could have been badly hurt . . .'

'Instead of just badly stupid?' teased Tyrone.

'Fuck off, you ugly knob!' replied Paula, pushing her braids back on her head.

RAJI AND SUKY MANN

Two weeks later . . .
Saturday 9 p.m.

Suky nudged his cousin Raji as the girl they were eyeing up leaned forward and gave them a good view of her cleavage.

'Dem tings is like footballs,' laughed Raji.

'She's fit – that's all I know,' said Suky, as the student sat back, saw him looking at her and looked away.

'That's the good thing about this place,' said Raji. 'Them student bitches are always in here.'

'Dutty too,' added Suky. 'One time me and Manj pulled three of 'em.'

Raji raised an eyebrow. 'Three?' he asked, impressed.

'Yeah, bro,' lied Suky. 'We had a party that night . . .'

'Fuck off!'

'Serious . . .'

They were sitting in the conservatory of The Horse, passing another Saturday night by getting drunk. Suky looked at the girl again. She was kissing some *gorah* knob now.

'Why them girls always pick the ugliest men?' he asked Raji.

'Who knows?' replied Raji. 'He's a white boy, innit – that's all them gal look for.'

Suky shook his head. 'That's 'cos they ain't tried no Desi, you get me?' he said.

'An' wit' your ugly face, they ain't goin' to neither,' laughed Raji.

Suky told his cousin to get lost and turned to look out of the window. As soon as he saw them he turned to his cousin.

'Bro – we got company,' he said quickly.

Raji turned to see who his cousin was on about and noticed Tyrone, Dean and David walking past the pub.

'They's walkin' by,' he told Suky.

'Let's see,' replied Suky.

They waited a few moments and then Suky walked round to the main part of the pub and stood in the doorway between it and the conservatory. Dean and David were chatting to some girls by the bar. Tyrone was getting drinks. Suky went back to his cousin.

'They're round the other side,' he told Raji.

'You wanna go round there – see what a gwaan?' asked Raji.

Suky shook his head. 'Nah – we gotta be cleverer than that,' he told him. 'Let's go outside and wait in the car . . .'

'What we gonna do in the car?'

Suky grinned. 'Trust me,' he said, finishing his bottle of Holsten Pils and getting up. He eyed the white girl one more time but she gave him a dirty look and turned away.

'Fucking *goreeh* slag,' he muttered, heading out of the conservatory exit into the car park.

David

Saturday 10.30 p.m.

I watched Dean do his best to try and pull the girls we were talking to. They weren't having it though. One of them kept on telling Dean that although she thought he was cute, she didn't go out with babies.

'How you know I'm too young?' he asked, still grinning.

'I can just tell,' said the girl. 'I can see it in your face.'

'I'm nineteen,' he lied to her.

'Yeah and I'm the Queen,' she replied, shaking her head.

'Well, at least buy us a drink,' he asked.

'See – now I know you ain't a man,' she told him, turning away to her friend.

Dean looked at me and Tyrone. 'You could have backed me up,' he said to us.

'And look as stupid as you?' I asked. 'Forget that.'

'You did a good enough job on yer own,' said Tyrone. 'They was *well* impressed – no *really*, they was . . .'

'My own cousin.' Dean grinned. '*Et tu Brute* . . .'

'*What?*' I asked.

'It's from *Julius Caesar*,' Tyrone told me.

'Yeah – *that* clears it all up,' I said.

Dean laughed. 'Thick bastard! You should read more.'

'And turn into *you*?' I asked. 'Maybe not.'

'Could be worse,' he said, shrugging. 'You could turn into you.'

I told him to fuck off and looked around the pub, wondering whether our dads were in. They had gone out for the night too.

'You reckon the old boys are in here?' I asked Dean.

'Nah – they were going to go into town.'

Tyrone shook his head. 'Best call out the army then,' he said.

'There's some old-time reggae dance on,' Dean told us. 'Mum's well pissed off because they didn't take her.'

'Yeah, but she's gone out with my mum,' I pointed out.

'They'll probably end up at the same place,' laughed Tyrone.

'No doubt,' said Dean. 'Getting drunk and arguin' . . .'

'That's why Simmy couldn't come out,' said Tyrone.

'Yeah – she got babysittin' duty – Lisa and Paula are round there.'

Dean laughed. 'Paula's seein' a lot of your sister nowadays,' he said.

'Like someone else I know,' I replied, winking at Tyrone.

'Yeah, yeah – take the piss,' replied Tyrone.

'I wasn't doin' that,' I said. 'And anyway – I thought you were supposed to go round and see her tonight?'

'Yeah – I'm goin' in a minute. She wanted Jay to go to bed first,' he said.

I shook my head. 'You ain't got a hope in hell,' I told him. 'Whenever my parents go out he stays up as long as he can.'

'I'll bribe him,' Tyrone suggested.

'Yeah and what about Paula and Lisa?' asked Dean.

'Them too,' he said.

'Although I know someone else who could bribe that Lisa many times as he wanted, you get me?' added Dean, with a wink.

'Fuck off!' I said, knowing that he was talking about me.

'She don't give me them sweet smiles like she gives you,' said Dean. 'Girl is in love wit' you, bro.'

I shook my head and finished my drink.

'Another one?' asked Dean.

'Yeah . . .' I said.

'What about you, Ty?'

Tyrone shook his head. 'Nah – I'm gone,' he told us.

'You'd better be too,' I said. 'Otherwise my sister is gonna kill you.'

Tyrone grinned and told us to behave ourselves.

'I'm tryin', bro,' replied Dean. 'I just gotta find the right gal to behave myself *with*.'

SUKY AND RAJI MANN

Saturday 11.10 p.m.

'Take a right here,' Raji told his cousin.

Suky looked at Raji in disgust. 'I grew up round here,' he said. 'Like I don't know my way around . . .'

'Just sayin',' explained Raji.

Suky drove slowly down the street, avoiding a pothole that was so deep it went all the way down to the old cobbled surface. At the end of the road he turned left and pulled up.

'He should be passing by here any minute,' said Raji. 'Ain't no other way he can go . . .'

Suky nodded and put the car into neutral, pulled the handbrake up and released the clutch. 'Best we wait then,' he replied.

Ten minutes later they saw him walking past, eating a kebab as he went.

'Look at that fuckin' monkey dropping his food every-where,' laughed Raji.

'What do you expect, bro?' asked Suky.

'Let me go get him,' said Raji.

Suky shook his head. 'Not on the main road – you wanna get done?'

They waited another few minutes and then set off again, shadowing him like he was prey. Which he was.

Five minutes later Suky saw him turn up another side street.

'This is the one,' he told Raji. 'You ready?'

Raji laughed. 'This time I am,' he said.

'Got the t'ing?'

'Yeah . . .'

Suky nodded. 'Wait until I pull up and then be quick.'

'No worries . . .'

TYRONE

Saturday 11.35 p.m.

Tyrone heard the car tyres screeching as he stuffed the last bit of his doner kebab into his mouth. It all happened so quickly he couldn't even turn round. Something cracked against the right side of his head and sent him flying. He dropped his kebab, hit a parked car and slid to the ground. Sweat had already broken out on his forehead, cold and nauseating. He looked at his attacker, saw him lift the baseball bat and bring it down against his shoulder. And then another strike to his face. The pain made him puke up large chunks of doner meat. He tried to get up but the pain was unbearable. His attacker called him a load of names and then got into the car, which sped away.

He used one hand to get out his mobile and another to hold the side of his head. The pain was sharp still and a throbbing had started too. He pushed the dial button when he got to Dean's number and put the phone to his ear, as the sweating got worse. There was no reply. He lay back on the ground now, looking up at a lamppost, wondering who else to call. Then the light above his head began to sway and blur. He closed his eyes and sucked in air . . .

The hands lifted him from the ground and put him on something solid that moved. He felt himself being lifted again, this time along with whatever he was lying on. Then a door slammed shut, followed by another. He tried to move his hands but couldn't. Something was securing them. He heard a voice above his head to his right.

'Stay awake, Tyrone . . . stay awake . . .'

He struggled to do what the voice wanted, opening and closing his eyes until finally he couldn't open them again. Then he felt everything go blank, including the pain . . .

DAVID

I scrabbled around on my bedside table, trying to find my phone. For a moment I thought that I'd been dreaming about it buzzing, only it wasn't a dream. I didn't know who was calling me at four in the morning and I didn't care. They were going to get a serious load of abuse. But when I answered the phone any thoughts of swearing at the caller disappeared. It was Dean and he sounded desperate.

'They got Tyrone,' he shouted.

'Huh?'

I shook my head to clear my thoughts. I was still half asleep.

'They bust him up bad—'

'Who?'

'Them Desi bastards!'

'Dean – hold on a minute . . .'

I sat up and tried to pay more attention.

'This is it now!' he shouted. 'All bets off this time. Them fucking Pak— I mean Asians gonna pay . . .'

I didn't get angry at the way Dean had nearly called Tyrone's attackers Pakis. I knew he was fuming. I would have been the same myself. But how did he know that it was the Desi Posse who attacked his cousin? I asked him.

'He told me—'

'Have the police spoken to him?' I asked.

'Yeah – but he didn't tell them shit,' admitted Dean.

'Where are you?' I asked.

'The hospital.'

'Is he gonna be OK?'

'Yeah, but he looks terrible – they did him with a baseball bat. Mashed up his head and shoulder. Cracked his cheekbone.'

'Shit . . .'

'He wants you to tell Simran,' Dean said.

'Yeah – she was fuming last night when he didn't show – said he weren't answering his phone. I know why now.'

'Just wake her and tell her,' insisted Dean. 'My old man is here too – he says he'll come get her.'

'OK – I'll call you back in ten minutes,' I told him.

I jumped out of bed and went to tell my sister. She answered on the fifth knock and when I went in she looked well pissed off.

'What the hell do you want?' she moaned.

'It's Tyrone – he's in hospital,' I said.

If I hadn't been so tired I probably would have tried to

tell her gently but I didn't. She looked at me in horror and then sat up.

'What . . . how?' she stammered.

Our voices must have woken my dad because the next thing I knew he was in the room asking us what was happening. When I told him he shook his head and told me to call Dean back.

'I'll go with her,' he said.

'But you're probably still pissed from your night out,' I warned.

'I'm fine and this isn't the time,' he snapped, going back into his room to get dressed.

Simran got out of bed and told me to let her get dressed too.

'I'll come with you,' I said.

She nodded. There were tears running down her face and I gave her a hug.

'He'll be OK,' I told her, getting angry myself.

SIMRAN

Sunday 4 p.m.

The nurse changed Tyrone's drip, telling me that I should go home and rest, just like they do on telly. I yawned. 'I'm OK,' I replied.

She smiled at me. 'He won't come to for a while – the painkillers will make him very sleepy. By the time he wakes up it'll be night.'

'I'll stay a bit longer,' I said.

Tyrone's parents were due back around five p.m. and I wanted to be there when they arrived. I looked at Tyrone's face, swollen all down one side, with two huge gashes in it. His right cheek was so swollen that it stuck out almost as much as his nose. I wanted to wake him up and kiss him, tell him that I was there, but I couldn't. He was in a bad way and needed to rest. So instead, I sat where I was and wondered whether our relationship was worth this. It had brought us nothing but grief since it started. Was it really worth nearly dying for something that so many people thought was wrong?

It took me about fifteen minutes to stop thinking that way and by then I was crying again. I couldn't understand why anyone would hurt another human being in such a way. What happened to their humanity, their conscience, when they hit someone with a baseball bat, knowing that it could kill them? What did it make them feel – pride, honour, satisfaction? It was just so warped.

Dean was at the hospital when I arrived, and after I had seen Tyrone, he took me to one side and told me what had happened. Tyrone had woken briefly, enough to speak to the police. Only he hadn't seen who hurt him. It happened so quickly that he didn't even have time to react. Dean told me that the police were on to it but I had the feeling that he was holding something back from me. I knew in my heart that it was the Desi Posse who had beaten up Tyrone. It had to be. It would have been too much of a coincidence otherwise. And I don't believe in coincidences. Everything happens for a reason, no matter how strange it is.

When I asked Dean if it had been the DP, he shrugged and looked away. Then he looked back and told me not to worry about it.

'If it was them – then they're dealt with, believe . . .' he said.

'But if you go after them, things will just get worse,' I argued.

Dean shrugged again. 'Worse than this?' he asked. 'That's my blood lying there – I ain't leavin' it.'

'It'll just keep going on and on,' I said, begging him to leave it alone, but Dean just shook his head.

'This is different,' he told me. 'It ain't like they just smacked him about a bit — they could have killed him. Someone has got to stop them fools before they do kill a man.'

'But that's the police — that's their job,' I pleaded.

'Fat chance of that,' replied Dean, before telling me to go back to the ward.

'Where are you going?' I asked.

'To talk to your brother,' he told me. 'And have a fag . . .'

Back in the side room where they were keeping Tyrone I saw my dad talking to Uncle Mikey and Tyrone's dad.

'They're gonna go after the people that did this,' I told them. 'David and Dean . . .'

'No they aren't,' said Uncle Mikey sternly. 'This ends right now.'

Tyrone's dad stood up and added his agreement too. 'I don't care what's happened,' he said. 'From now on — this is over.'

My dad eyed me suspiciously. 'Do you know something, Sim?' he asked.

'Tyrone's been getting grief from an Asian gang at school,' I admitted.

'For going out with you?' asked Uncle Mikey.

'Yeah, but they had a beef before that too.'

'The fight outside the school . . .' said my dad.

'That big gang thing?' asked Tyrone's dad.

I nodded. 'Tyrone was involved,' I told them all. 'He didn't start it – it was the Desi Posse—'

'The who?' asked his dad, looking confused.

'It's a long story,' I said, before telling them everything that had been going on.

It wasn't that I wanted to stitch up Tyrone, Dean and David. I just didn't want them to try and get revenge for Tyrone. That would make things worse.

SIMRAN

One week later

The hospital had let Tyrone go after two days but he was quite groggy and his face was still badly swollen. I'd been to see him every day and he'd even managed to start joking again, talking about how much he liked his new face. Sitting on the sofa, I smiled to myself at the thought of his stupid jokes just as David walked into the living room.

'What you grinning at, you weirdo?' he asked.

'Your face, your hair and mostly the way you think that those jeans go with that top,' I teased.

'Shut up, you cow,' he replied, sitting down opposite me.

'Where are Mum and Dad?'

'Out somewhere . . .'

'So it's you, me and the demon child from hell.'

'Yep,' replied David, turning on the telly.

'Aren't you going to ask me about Tyrone?' I said.

'No point,' he told me. 'You'll tell me anyway.'

'Knob . . .'

'I didn't know they'd hit him there,' joked my brother.

'Oh, don't be a twa—'

The doorbell rang just as I swore at him.

'Who's that?' he asked, looking pissed off.

'If you answer it, you'll find out,' I told him.

'You get it,' he said. 'I can't be arsed.'

'Yes you can,' I said, getting up. 'You *are* an arse . . .'

I walked into the hallway, opened the door and nearly fell over with shock. Uncle Malkit was standing in the doorway, and behind him was my grandad. My uncle looked me up and down in disgust and then spoke to his father.

'I'll be back at nine o'clock. Be ready,' he told him.

With that and another disgusted glance in my direction, Uncle Malkit walked back down the drive to his shiny new Mercedes penis extension. I looked at my grandad, waiting for the lecture to begin – maybe the odd swear word or two – but he just smiled at me and walked into the house.

'Making me the cup tea, daughter,' he said, in his funny English.

'Hi, Baba-ji,' I said, raising an eyebrow. 'How are you?'

'Can't complaining.' He grinned. 'Ju been the naughty girl though, innit?'

Here we go, I thought to myself, only for the old man to surprise me so much I nearly went into shock. Instead of telling me off he grinned again and then winked at me!

I showed him into the kitchen, where he sat down at the table and asked me where the boys were.

'Here's one of them,' I replied, as David came into the kitchen.

'*Gramps* – what you doin' here?' David asked.

'I come to kick your backside, boy,' replied Gramps.

'Very funny,' said David, giving me a look that said, *What the hell is going on here then?*

'Where is your dad?' he asked, this time in Punjabi.

'He's gone out with Mum,' I told him, also in Punjabi.

My grandad nodded and then motioned for me to come sit down. 'Good,' he said, continuing in his mother tongue. 'I wanted to talk to you two anyway.'

'Do you want me to drag Jay away from his computer?' asked David.

As he shook his head, I wondered who'd spiked up his short grey hair for him. It looked like he'd been using hair wax, the trendy old git. His clothes were good too – simple beige trousers and a nice cut to his white shirt. I was glad to see he wasn't wearing a shell suit like my uncle, although I wasn't too sure about his bright white trainers.

'Maybe later,' he told David. 'For now I want you to tell me what has been going on.'

'Well, for starters,' I began, in my best Punjabi, 'you're supposed to be on hunger strike—'

'*Heh?*'

I shook my head and smiled as he crossed and uncrossed his skinny legs.

'I knew it couldn't be true,' I told him, leaning across and kissing him on the cheek. 'You're too lovely to be like them . . .'

He shrugged. 'Let's see, shall we?' he said.

★ ★ ★

I told him everything, exactly as it had happened, including all the trouble with the Desi Posse and with my uncles. He sat and nodded his head every now and then but he didn't reply until I had finished. When I'd explained everything, he asked me if I was OK.

'Yes,' I said. 'Tyrone's much better now and I'm ignoring all the things they say to me at school.'

'Don't listen to them,' he told me. 'They're all stupid.'

I looked over at David to register my shock. I'd been expecting my grandad to have the same reaction as my uncles – not because I thought he was like them; because of what they had said. It had obviously all been a lie.

'Why didn't you come to see us,' I asked, 'after you found out? They told us that you were angry and that you wouldn't eat . . .'

He swore in Punjabi.

'Baba-ji!' I said, embarrassed.

'Sorry,' he replied. 'Now where's this cup of tea?'

Later on, as we sat in the living room, he told us a story about working on his market stall, way back in 1979, when my dad was nine. David and I sat and listened in wonder, like little kids do when you read to them, as Gramps told his tale.

CENTRAL POLICE
STATION, LEICESTER –
NOVEMBER 1979

Gulbir Singh gave the policeman a dirty look as he took in what he'd just been told.

'This ain't India,' continued the policeman, sneering in the same way the skinheads had done.

Gulbir had arrived at the police station with Mr Abbas to try and help the three black men who had come to their aid earlier in the evening. Over and over again he had told the police that the men they'd arrested had probably saved his life and that of Mr Abbas. But again and again he'd met a wall of indifference and outright racism. Even the head policeman, the one with all the stripes, had smirked and asked him when he was thinking of going back 'home'. Exasperated, Gulbir walked back to Mr Abbas and took a seat in the waiting area.

'What can you do,' asked Mr Abbas through a swollen jaw.

'Who knows?' replied Gulbir.

'They are the same as the NF,' added Mr Abbas. 'In uniforms . . .'

'They say that the *kaleh* started it and that they are going to press charges,' Gulbir told his friend.

'With which witness?' asked Mr Abbas. 'Anyone who saw can tell them what really happened.'

'We are no more than animals to them,' replied Gulbir bitterly. 'Whether we come from India, Pakistan or Jamaica.'

'*Inshallah* – if I had the words,' said Mr Abbas, 'I would tell them where they could go.'

Gulbir fought back an urge to smash the police station to pieces, the rage in his chest squeezing his heart like a powerful claw. 'What can we do?' he asked through clenched teeth.

It was forty minutes later that several fellow stall-holders arrived, most of them white men. Gulbir saw them walk in and raised an eyebrow. What was going on?

'Where are they, Mr Singh?' asked Mr Davis, whose second-hand stall stood three pitches down from Gulbir's.

'Who?' asked Gulbir.

'The black lads.'

In his broken English, Gulbir explained to the stall-holders what had happened since he'd arrived at the police station.

'Sod that,' exclaimed Mr Davis, marching over to the reception desk.

Gulbir watched as Mr Davis demanded to see the

person in charge and stood up, amazed, when his shouting and cursing made the man who had told Gulbir to go back 'home' hang his head and nod his consent. As the rest of the white stallholders added their testimony to what Mr Davis was saying, the head officer turned the colour of a beetroot and then, within ten minutes, the three black men were in the waiting area with them, free to go.

'That's one up his arse,' grinned Mr Davis, as Gulbir thanked him. 'Fascist stormtrooper . . .'

Outside, as snow began to fall in thick flakes, Gulbir opened the door to his van and ushered Mr Abbas and two of the black men in.

'Hurry,' he said. 'This weather will be the death of us.'

The taller of the two black men, who had said his name was Norris, grinned. 'Seen, Missa Singh. It too raas col' in dis yah country,' he said.

Gulbir smiled back, remembering the phrase he'd heard so many black men use – a thank-you maybe – not that he knew for sure that it was.

'Rass class . . .' he told Norris, unable to work out why Norris burst into laughter and clapped an arm around his shoulder.

'Easy, Missa Singh!'

Gulbir fired up his van and turned on the radio, as his son Mandip's favourite song, 'OK Fred', came on for maybe the fourth time that day. Gulbir smiled.

SIMRAN

'I learned a good lesson that day,' he told us as he finished his story. 'People are good or they are bad. Their colour isn't the important thing. It's what is in their hearts. Tell me, Simran, does this *kalah* of yours — does he have a good heart?'

I smiled and said that he did. The best.

'Then I am not angry. I am an old man and if I wanted my family to only mix with Indians I would have stayed in India. You are English children — that is the way things are. When I left India I did things my parents and my family did not wish of me — but I was young and the world was mine and I did what I wanted to do. You are the same and I won't take that from you. You're only here for a short time, *beteh*. Enjoy it . . .'

I stood up, went over to my grandad and gave him the biggest hug I had ever given anybody.

'Enough!' he said. 'You're crying on my new shirt.'

I smiled. 'I don't care.'

'Now, where is this son of mine and his lovely wife?' he said, picking up his mug. 'Any chance of next cup tea?' he added in English.

'Anything for you, Baba-ji,' I told him, taking the mug from his hand.

David grinned. 'What was the name of that song?' he asked Gramps.

'Which one?'

'Dad's favourite one.'

Gramps smiled. '"OK Fred",' he replied, in his heavily accented English.

'Do you know who it's by?' asked David.

'*Ki pattah?*' said Gramps, admitting that he didn't know.

David grinned again. 'No worries,' he told us, before running off upstairs, the nutter.

My parents turned up about an hour later and my dad was almost as surprised to see his father as I had been.

'What are you doing here?' he asked in Punjabi.

'You haven't been to see me,' said my grandad. 'So I thought I'd come to you—'

'But Malkit said that you were angry with us and—'

'I've already had this conversation with my grand-daughter,' he replied. 'She can tell you what I said. But ask yourself this, son. If I was angry with you, would I be here – drinking your expensive whisky?' Gramps winked at me.

'But you're not drinking whisky . . .' said my dad, falling into his trap.

'Only because you haven't offered me any,' he said.

My mum grinned and asked him if he was staying for dinner as Dad went to get his private stash of whisky.

'Malkit said he'd come and get me at nine,' replied Gramps. 'Although I don't really want him to . . .'

'Why don't you stay for a few days?' asked my mum.

'But what about my clothes?' he asked.

'I'll go and get them for you,' replied my mum. 'It'll be a pleasure . . .'

This time *she* winked at me. The chance to get one over on Aunt Pritam was too good to pass up.

'Why don't you call them now – tell them that you're staying,' added my mum. 'I'm sure they won't mind.'

Gramps eyed my mum with suspicion. 'Are you trying to shame Pritam?' he asked.

'No, no,' lied my mum.

'You should,' replied Gramps. 'She's an evil witch.'

We all burst into laughter as my dad returned with the whisky.

'What's so funny?' he asked, looking confused, as David came into the kitchen with a CD in his hands.

'Hey, Dad,' he said, putting the CD into the little player on the worktop. 'Remember this?'

As the song '*OK Fred*' began to filter through the speakers, Gramps grinned.

'Oh my God!' said my dad. 'Who told you about that?' But he was already looking at my gramps.

'Amazing what you can find on the Internet,' David told us.

SIMRAN

It took just five days for everything to turn to shit.

Tyrone had recovered enough to want to go out for a drink so I organized it. I rang Paula and told David and Dean that we'd meet at a Nando's restaurant and then go for a few drinks. They were up for it and by the Friday evening I was all happy. I rang Lisa too, and told her to come along. She jumped at the chance and came round to mine early so that we could do our hair and get dressed up. As we tried on different outfits, I had the giggles and I couldn't work out why. I think I was just happy, especially now I knew my grandad was on my side. It meant a lot to have him on board, although my uncles were still angry.

The police turned up at just after half-six in the evening, asking to speak to David and Dean. They'd been round to Dean's house first and Uncle Mikey had told them that he was at ours. When I heard all the commotion I went downstairs to find out what was going on. The police officers were in the living room, a man and a woman, and they were questioning the lads. I walked in as David denied that he'd done anything.

'So where were you last night?' asked the policeman.

'Out . . .' replied Dean, as the doorbell went again.

'What's going on?' I asked.

My mum told me to be quiet as the policewoman spoke up. I turned to see Dean's dad come in, a worried look on his face.

'What time were you out?' asked the policewoman.

'I dunno,' said David. 'Went out 'bout seven and got in round eleven – why?'

'Were you anywhere near Evington Valley Road – the youth club?' asked the man.

'Nah – we was over by Queen's Road an' that,' replied Dean.

I looked at them both, convinced they were making it up. They seemed to know what to say to every question. But I still didn't know what had happened.

'Will somebody tell me what's going on?' I insisted.

'Two lads got badly beaten up – Raji Mann and Pally Johal,' Dean told me. 'An' they think we did it.'

'No we don't,' said the woman. 'We're just following a line of inquiry.'

'You've had some trouble with them though, haven't you? We spoke to the youth workers—' added the man.

'To Kevin, you mean,' replied David. 'Fuckin' grass—'

'*David!*' shouted my mum.

'What would he grass you up over?' asked the woman. 'If you've done nothing wrong, then—'

'I was talking about the fight we had with Raji and them,' cut in David. 'But that don't mean shit.'

'We was over Clarendon Park way,' said Dean. 'Went to check some girls . . . ask them . . .'

The policeman looked at his colleague.

'Do you have names and addresses for them?' asked the woman.

'Course,' replied Dean, telling her.

The police officers asked a few more questions and then left, saying that they might need to talk to the lads again. When they had gone my dad turned to David and Dean.

'Was it you?' he asked.

'*No!*' protested David. 'We didn't touch them . . .'

'Are you sure?' asked Uncle Mikey.

'We was with them girls,' said Dean. 'Man – you two are worse than them coppers.'

'If I find out it was you,' warned Dean's dad, 'both of you are in some deep shit.'

'It wasn't us,' repeated David. 'They probably mouthed off to the wrong people – they're always gettin' into shit.'

'OK,' said Dean's dad.

The lads left the room and I followed them up the stairs.

'It was you, wasn't it?' I said to David.

'No – I told you,' he replied, although he couldn't look me in the face.

'How bad are they?' I asked.

'Dunno,' said Dean. 'I heard someone today say that they're in intensive care – 'bout as bad as what they did to Tyrone, I hope.'

'Great,' I said. 'Now their mates are gonna think you had something to do with it.'

'Why?' asked David.

'Think about it,' I told them. 'Tyrone gets beat up after having beef with the DP and then two of them get battered just under two weeks later—'

'Let 'em think what they like,' said Dean. 'I ain't scared of them, man.'

I shook my head and went into my bedroom, where Lisa wanted to know what had happened. I told her as I pulled on the fitted white shirt I'd bought a few months earlier. I hadn't worn it yet.

'Wow!' said Lisa. 'That's lovely. Those flowers are great.'

'Should I wear it?' I asked.

'Yeah! It really suits your skin colour.'

'That's what the girl in the shop said,' I told her.

'She was right,' replied Lisa.

It happened as we were crossing London Road to go to The Horse for last orders. I was holding Tyrone's free hand and talking to Paula about something – I can't remember what now, but then again I don't remember too much about that night. Lisa was chatting up my brother and Dean was teasing them. Paula ran across to avoid a passing car, leaving me and Tyrone standing just off the pavement. He let go of my hand and grabbed me around the waist. Then he kissed me and told me that he loved me. I kissed him back and smiled. I remember Paula shouting at us, telling us to hurry up because she wanted a drink. Then I remember David, Dean and Lisa running across too. There were about three cars coming so me and Tyrone waited a bit longer and he kissed me again . . .

I turned to look both ways before crossing, and although there was a car about thirty metres away, it was crawling along. I remember that it didn't have its lights on – I was thinking the driver was stupid. Then Tyrone grabbed my hand and we began to walk across. But I dropped my bag and stopped to pick it up. Tyrone stopped with me; only he was standing a couple of metres away.

'Come on, Sim,' he said to me, grinning.

As I grabbed my bag, I was thinking how beautiful he was. Then I heard tyres squeal and turned to see the car with no lights heading straight for Tyrone. Everything seemed to slow right down. I could see it coming and I ran forward and pushed Tyrone out of the way. In my head now, when my attempts at forgetting fail, I think that I turned round and saw the face of the driver, but I can't have . . .

The car hit me full on in the side. I heard myself scream just before it hit me and then everything went quiet . . .

DAVID

My dad drove my grandad to Uncle Malkit's house, where they picked him and Uncle Rajbir up and brought them back to the hospital. I was sitting in a waiting area, with Mum, Lisa and Tyrone. Dean was outside with his parents and his sister. Lisa was crying so I held onto her and told her that it would be OK. But I didn't know it would be. My sister was broken like a china cup that had fallen to the floor. The car had thrown her into the air and almost to the other side of the road. I ran to help her, and saw that her legs were at weird angles to her body and one of the bones in her right arm had broken through the skin. Her head was deeply gashed and she was unconscious.

My mum was sitting with Tyrone and he had his arms around her, like a little boy. He was still crying. He hadn't stopped. My mum was the same and both of them just sat there and held each other.

The driver had lost control of the car after it hit Simran and ploughed into a parked BMW. Dean had been the first one to the hit-and-run car. He told me that he'd got to the car and then stopped in shock. The driver was my cousin Satnam, Uncle Rajbir's younger son. My own *cousin* and Ruby's *brother*. The passenger, who'd been thrown through the windscreen and onto the bonnet, was Suky Mann.

When my dad arrived he stood at the entrance to the waiting room with his two brothers. Simran was still in surgery. I looked up at my dad and he wiped away tears. Then he turned to his brothers and spoke in a voice loud enough for everyone to hear.

'Look at him,' he said, gesturing towards Tyrone. 'What's so bad about him that you hate him so much? He's just like you and me – just like my son . . . a human being . . .'

My uncles looked away in shame as my grandad came to join me.

'Are you happy now?' asked my dad. 'Now that my daughter is lying in a hospital – more dead than alive. And for what? Because you can't see past the colour of a man's skin . . .'

'We didn't know—' began Uncle Malkit.

'*Shut up!*' shouted my dad. 'Do you think I care? All your poison, all your shit – was it worth it? If my daughter dies you'll pay for the rest of your lives. No amount of money and cars and false pride will help you – I swear it on the Guru Granth . . .'

My uncles looked around at us all. If they were hoping

to find any kind of sympathy in that room they were mistaken. Even when Uncle Malkit offered to take my grandad home to bed, he got no joy.

'I'd rather sleep in the park,' replied my gramps. 'Get out of here if you've got any shame left.'

SIMRAN

It's taken me twelve months to even begin to try walking. I have to be held up between two poles that I use to try and haul myself along. It's painful and it's hard but Tyrone comes with me every time, which makes it a bit easier. And him being there makes me even more determined.

I'm trying to put the thought of the car out of my mind too but it's really hard. The point just before it hit me, when I looked into the face of the driver and saw my own cousin. Satnam is in prison now, along with Suky Mann, and I really don't feel any guilt for testifying against him. I still can't believe what he did. It makes me angry because I was so happy and I wanted to do my exams and go to college and music festivals and have a normal life. He took all that away from me and he can rot.

I *will* go to college though, and I'll go travelling and

do all the things I've always dreamed of. And I won't be doing them in a wheelchair either. For the first six months the doctors said I wouldn't feel my legs again and they were wrong. Then they said I wouldn't walk again, and guess what, they're going to be wrong about that too. Every day I do a bit more on my own – just a little bit more. It's my only goal for the next twelve months or so – walking.

David and Lisa are going out with each other. That boy that Lisa had been upset over, a few weeks before what happened – that had been my brother! The dirty cow! They seem really good together too and they've been so supportive of me, but I wouldn't have expected anything less from them. Gramps has moved in with my parents. He gave my dad a load of money and told him to convert the loft into a room. That's David's new room and Gramps is in his old one. I like having him around. He tells me funny stories and whenever he sees Tyrone he calls out '*raas claas*', which he thinks is a greeting. Tyrone hasn't got the heart to tell him it isn't – that it's actually quite a rude thing to say, calling someone an 'arse cloth'. Instead he nods and replies, '*Sat Sri Akaal*,' which is Punjabi for hello. David taught him how to say it.

Tyrone and my dad also sing me songs when they come visit me in hospital. I have to go in all the time for various little things. I'm always laughing at Tyrone because he can't sing at all, and what's worse is that he eggs the old man on. If Tyrone is bad, my dad is, like, super-bad – although I think he'd like it if I called him that. It drives my mum mad and she reckons that's why her hair turned grey all over. But I don't believe her. It was all the stress and the sorrow and the pain, and I want her to dye it back to brown but she won't. She says she feels dignified – like a lady – until I point out that it isn't dignified to eat ham, banana and ice-cream sandwiches, which she loves. Then she just swears at me.

We're all OK, which is the main thing. All doing fine apart from me, and I'm getting there. It's gonna take a while but it's going to happen and then I'm gonna take Tyrone's black hand and put it in my own brown hand and walk down the street with him. And we're going to hold our heads up high. And you know what – if they don't like it, who cares? It's hardly like the last taboo, is it?

ABOUT THE AUTHOR

Bali Rai is so busy writing and visiting schools that he didn't have time to write his own author notes. From what we can tell, he still lives in Leicester, still goes on trips all over Europe and is much better at getting out of bed on time.

He's still not married, either, although there were rumours about a dancer, Las Vegas, a chapel and a preacher dressed as Elvis, pretending to be Bob Marley. As yet these rumours are still that – and to be honest we think he made them up himself.

The Last Taboo is his fifth novel for Corgi and if he can actually get any writing done we may soon get another one. Until then you can always see what he gets up to at **www.balirai.com**.

(UN)ARRANGED MARRIAGE

Manny is a Punjabi boy from Leicester and he doesn't want to get married . . . Bali Rai's stunning debut novel about generational gulfs and cultural differences within family and society.

'Absorbing and engaging . . . a highly readable debut from Bali Rai that teenagers of any culture will identify with'   *Observer*
978 0 552 54734 5

RANI & SUKH

Rani and Sukh have just started going out together. But Rani is a Sandhu and Sukh is a Bains – and sometimes names can lead to serious trouble . . . A gripping novel that sweeps the reader from modern-day Britain to the Punjab in the 1960s and back again in a ceaseless cycle of tragedy and conflict.

'Overwhelmingly powerful'   *The Bookseller*
978 0 552 54890 8

THE CREW

When you live in the concrete heart of a major UK city and someone leaves a bag full of cash in the alley behind your house you had best leave it alone. It's got to be bad news – after all, what kind of people leave fifteen grand lying around?

'A jewel of a book'   *Independent*   978 0 552 54739 0

THE WHISPER

The Crew didn't think things could ever get that bad again. They were dead wrong. Someone's grassing up the dealers and the whisper on the street says it's Nanny and the Crew – they need to act fast before the situation explodes . . .

'Exhilarating sequel to the crew . . . unflinching and authentic'
Publishing News   978 0 552 54891 5